W9-AFF-425

Advanced praise for

Ship Shapely:

A Gil Yates Private Investigator Novel

"Wit great wit and high style, Boyle offers a wonderfully comic, mixed metaphor-spouting hero who combines awkward charm with cunning instinct—a mix of Austin Powers, James Bond, and Sam Spade. Fun reading."

—*ALA Booklist*

"Gil's as charming as ever."

—*Kirkus Reviews*

"A clever plot coupled with a lively protagonist."

—*Library Journal*

"...wry cynicism and quirky humor. In a genre with a recent habit of explicit cruelty and violence, Boyle's light comic mystery is, as Gil Yates would say, 'a different kettle of gefeltefish entirely'."

—*ForeWord Magazine*

SHIP SHAPELY

A Gil Yates Private Investigator Novel

Alistair Boyle

ALLEN A. KNOLL, PUBLISHERS
Santa Barbara, CA

Allen A. Knoll, Publishers, 200 West Victoria Street,
Santa Barbara, CA 93101-3627

Printed in the United States of America

05 04 03 02 01 00 5 4 3 2

Library of Congress Cataloging-in-Publication Data

Boyle, Alistair.
Ship shapely : a Gil Yates private investigator novel / Alistair Boyle. - -1st ed.
p. cm.
ISBN 1-888310-99-5 (alk. paper)
I. Title.
PS3552.0917S55 1999
813'.54--dc21 99-23574
CIP

text typeface is ITC Galliard, 12 point
Printed on 60-pound Lakewood white, acid free paper
Case bound with Kivar 9, Smyth Sewn

Also by Alistair Boyle

Bluebeard's Last Stand
The Unlucky Seven
The Con
The Missing Link

Drop-dead gorgeous they were. Five young women, fair of face and exquisite of body. He'd hired them to do his bidding, but he didn't pay them anything. There they were before me in bashful bikinis, more or less—well, not in person, but in photographs swimming on the coffee table in front of his widow and me. The pix left little to the imagination.

They were drop-dead gorgeous all right, but he's the one who had dropped dead.

He may have had some help crossing over to permanent dreamland from one or more of those beauties who were doing his bidding. His widow thought so.

He, being Les Quincy, was a guy we could all learn from. What, after all, did he have to offer these nicely constructed young ladies? It had to be more than his curious sleeping arrangements.

The sun was on a roaring drunk outside in Santa Fe, New Mexico, but the widow Quincy had a fortuitous adobe fortress with walls as thick as my beloved wife's hide. I speak of Tyranny Rex of whom more later—when you are in the skipping mode.

In the center of the neatly arranged photographs was the ad. It was what suckered the fems into the fix in the first place.

> Women to man 35' sailboat for tour of Pacific. Must be in excellent physical condition. No experience necessary. Room and board. Send recent photo to Box 1492, Honolulu, HI 96809

What an intriguing juxtaposition of words—women to man. I didn't realize it then, but there was a nefarious hidden meaning there.

Edna Quincy was a sad-eyed woman, who had turned a blind eye to a lot of stuff her late husband had pulled. Though he was, according to all reports, swimming with Davy Jones at present, my sense was she still loved him. Otherwise, how to account for her eagerness to invest in an investigation of her husband's death—a year after the authorities had ruled it an accident?

Her place was furnished like a high-end hotel, with brocade scenes of the French countryside on whitish maple would-be antiques.

There was a chest after Louis something and a pot that had the potential for holding umbrellas, or perhaps horsewhips; a copy from the Han Dynasty.

Mrs. Quincy sat on the couch beside me, her

hind quarters smothering the hind quarters of the quarter horses engaged in fox hunting on the couch fabric. Her hands were clasped in her lap, and she stared with an unblinking gaze that put you in mind of one of those bygone soaps where some pure-hearted woman was pining for some no-good fella who was bound to bring her grief.

Edna Quincy had suffered her grief and now she was attempting to put it behind her. That's why I was here (at her expense) to solve the mystery once and for all time. The mystery of how her husband had met his untimely demise.

The funny thing was I could picture Edna in one of those eensy-weensy-teensy bikinis. Though her skin said she hadn't been outdoors in a century, there were suggestions in her simple flowered frock that things were not in bad repair. Her cheekbones gave her face a badly needed uplift, and her shellacked hair was blond and as lively as a dead polecat.

But she was a woman with a cause, and I liked women with causes as long as they didn't get too pushy.

"He ran that ad only once for each trip," she said, with a morose twang, as though she were singing bluegrass. "That's all he needed. Never failed to pull hundreds of responses from lonely women. Didn't matter to them they weren't even getting paid. It was an adventure, I suppose."

"You ever go on one of his sailing trips?"

"Oh, no. He didn't want that. This was *his* thing, you see."

"Well, but...didn't it bother you? His going on a ship with all these beauties?"

She looked away. It was answer enough.

"How was he able to afford these trips? Didn't he have a job?"

"Oh, yes. He was a flagpole painter. It was good money," she said, as though she weren't certain.

"Tell me the truth..." I prodded.

She look at me with new respect. Then she dropped her eyes. "I inherited a little," she said so softly I wouldn't have heard if I hadn't said the words to myself as she was saying them.

"So you underwrote his...well, philandering, I guess?"

She nodded, and it took no little effort to move her head on that plane.

"He was a charming man, my Les," she said, her eyes drifting from their moorings. "He charmed *everything* right off me."

"Where did you meet?"

"I was working in the federal office building in L.A. He came to paint the flagpole. Swept me off my feet, he did. He was so charming. And virile. His pores oozed a kind of animalism, you know. His body was...if I said perfect would you think me a fool?" I opened my mouth to protest but she went on. "It's not hard for me to see how he could get those young girls to fawn all over him." There was enough sadness in her distant gaze to float a homeless shelter on Saturday night.

"Les could turn on the charm all right. Said I was beautiful, one in a million. Made my head spin. There aren't that many guys who can sling it like he did. I wanted to believe it, so I did.

"I should have had some suspicion, I guess. I look back and realize I must have told him about my inheritance. I have a big mouth. Secretly, I thought it would make me attractive to him. My grandfather made a killing in pork bellies. I don't even know what they are, but it sounds ridiculous. I just always wondered why it couldn't be something more socially acceptable—like cattle. Pigs," she said, making a sour face.

My question was, had she inherited enough to pay my exorbitant contingency fee? Or should I nickel and dime her like the run of the mill P.I.s—so much a day plus expenses?

"One of them did it," she said pointing to the menagerie of pictures on the table. Looking wistfully at those bronzed bodies, I could easily imagine this would have been one of my most enjoyable gigs. "They all said they saw him at night, but by morning he was gone. It was off the Hawaiian Islands. The coroner ruled accidental drowning, but they don't have his body." She sniffled a little. Could have been an allergy.

"What makes you think these girls would tell me a different story than they told the coroner?"

"Oh, I don't know. I just heard about you from a friend who works at Softex—I thought it was worth a try. I mean, if you found that nut who was blowing those people to bits with his mailed bombs, I thought it was worth a shot, that's all."

She was speaking of my chronicle, *The Unlucky Seven*. "I worked for Harold Mattlock there," I said. "He's one of the richest men in the world. I told you on the phone I didn't come cheap—but if I didn't get the turkey, you didn't pay the plumber."

"Contingency," she nodded. I couldn't tell if the dull nod meant she understood, agreed or resigned herself to my *modus*. That's from *modus operandi*, a Latin phrase meaning method of operation. I love to use pretentious words whenever humanly possible. I learned that from my father-in-law, Elbert A. Wemple, high potentate of Elbert A. Wemple and Associates, Realtors. And a more pretentious bag of bones you'd never hope to meet. It is under his fat thumb I have labored, more or less legitimately, ever since the instant I said "I do" vis-à-vis his daughter, Dorcas, the glass blower, whom I affectionately (more or less) refer to as Tyranny Rex.

"I was hoping you'd make an exception," she purred like a kitten on the couch.

"What did you have in mind?" It was a question I didn't have to ask. I knew what she had in mind. And it wasn't my pick of the bikinied litter on the table. It was rather Sears prices for Cartier workmanship.

"Well, I thought...maybe this once...you could work like a regular investigator."

"A thousand a day and expenses," I said, raising an eyebrow.

"A thou?" she choked on the amount.

"There are lot of guys..."

"I know," she said waving her hand in front of my face. "I want you."

I suppose that was flattering. It would have been if she hadn't quibbled with my price.

"What's your rock bottom...?"

"I told you I only do contingency. But if I succeed it comes high."

"Like the shyster lawyers," she said. It wasn't a question.

"It may seem easy on the surface," I said, "but what you want might be next to impossible. The case has already been investigated by professionals. If one of these..." I waved at the photos "...cuties *is* a murderess, there isn't the slightest cause to imagine she will break down and confess it to me—*and* the authorities, with the prospect of sitting in jail for the rest of her life. It's only in the movies that people break down and spill the legumes."

"So, shouldn't you be happier with a…modest fee?"

"Ah," I said. "Modest. That's the key word." In my other life, I thought, as a property managing drudge south of the thumb of Daddybucks Wemple, I was modest enough. As Gil Yates, Private Eye, I was a dashing, daring, sexy sleuth without a modest bone in my skeleton—especially not when it came to charging for my services.

"How much is it worth to you?" I said, laying my cards out with the china and silverware. I know that cliché isn't quite right, but I have this blind spot about clichés—I always screw them up.

"A lot more than I can pay, I'm afraid."

"Why? Why do you care? It's been almost a year. Why did you wait? These things have a way of going cold."

"The police were working on it," she said without cheer. "I had hopes…"

"They closed the case?"

She nodded, sadness all over her.

"Can't let it go?"

She shook her head. "I tried, believe me."

"Is it vengeance—retribution—curiosity—tidiness? Perhaps you should temper that with what you're willing to spend on the project."

"I just want to know," she sounded muffled, as though she were under a rock—and in a way I expect she was.

"But in a way you do know," I said. "Accidental drowning."

She shook her head. "Les was a world-class swimmer. He could have swum from Honolulu to L.A. No way did he drown swimming."

"Maybe he had a heart attack in the water?"

She shook her head again. "What would he be doing in the ocean after dark? After everyone had gone to sleep? That's the story," she said. "I say at least one of the girls knows something she isn't telling. The police didn't seem to care."

"Why do you think that is?"

She shrugged. "Laziness—or..."

"Or what?"

She didn't answer right away. She seemed to be getting in touch with her thoughts.

"Les could be abrasive," she said, as though she were making a concession to her own deluded memory. "He made some enemies."

"You mean someone else may have gotten to him?"

"The girls say not," Edna Quincy threw up her hands, "but if they were all asleep?"

I sat there rubbing my chin. It was a thoughtful pose I'd picked up somewhere—maybe from that slab of flab my father-in-law. But what was I thinking? This was a no-winner if I ever saw one. As far as I could see, she had no financial stake in the outcome. She wasn't going to get x-million if I proved it was murder—the death certificate called it accidental—no suicide mentioned. So where would my windfall come in?

"Please help me," she pleaded, with eyes the size

of baseball plates. I wasn't in the charity business. I also subscribed to the received wisdom that no good deed went unpunished. So, why didn't I head for the nearest exit?

Well, I thought, the idea was not without its advantages. The most obvious was lying on the table before me. Five of the most gorgeous creatures you ever hoped to lay eyes on.

Then, subsidiarily, I would have to go to Hawaii to talk to the bureaucrats there—and Hawaii, specifically the University of, was where my daughter, Felicity, was enjoying the umpteenth year of her education, if you can call it that. The upside of that was that Daddypimple, Felicity's engorged grandfather, was footing her endless bills. (No way could I have afforded it before I limed onto this P.I. racket—and when I started to pepper away some dough I didn't see any need to broadcast it to you-know-who.)

I hadn't seen Felicity in a long time—she was adroit at staying away from home—and who can blame her? An excuse to see her without the encumbrance of Tyranny Rex had a certain appeal. Felicity was so unlike me that I was always baffled in her presence. Though I really had no legitimate basis to question my paternity.

I sensed she thought I was dithering. She sucked in some air and seemed to be playing her ace.

"Oh," she said. "I have a copy of a letter one of the girls sent her boyfriend. If you take the case, I'll give it to you."

"How about letting me see it? It could help me decide."

She sighed. After an eternity was dead and buried, she hoisted herself, disappeared through a door and after a dramatic pause, long enough to give me hunger pains, she came back with a single sheet of paper. She looked at it briefly, not long enough to read anything, then handed it to me.

I looked from her to the paper. It was written in a tiny, girly hand that was juvenile flowery—I's dotted with daisies, O's in the shape of hearts when the spirit moved her—T's were unmistakable crosses, set off as though they were on Calvary Mountain. The paper was lined tablet, a slight cut above newsprint.

Dear Mark,

I pray to God that you and He will forgive me for this grievous mistake. I feel like Lot's wife: one wrong turn and I'll be turned into a pillar of salt. And wrong turns seem to be all there are here.

Captain Les, which is what he wants us to call him, is not your idea of a Christian gentleman. He is a heathen and a lecher and he expects all of us to take turns sharing his bed. Imagine! Perhaps the thing that surprises me most is not his lechery, but that the other girls seem to be okay with it. He is a conceited dictator and repulses me. He has let me know in no uncertain terms when it is my turn, it's that or sleep on the deck. He is leaving me for last to give me plenty of time to make up my mind. I told him I didn't need more time, my mind was already made up. Deck, here I come.

Sometimes when I feel better than I

do now I have to laugh at myself and all the reasons I wanted to come on this trip. I'm just out of college with nothing really to do, and I thought it was a lark. A real travel adventure— see the world and all. And when I interviewed, Captain Les seemed an alright guy. He was interested in me and all. Didn't talk about sex—hardly at all. I thought I could fend him off by just saying no. But now I see another side to him.

He's certainly no intellect. His reading matter runs to Penthouse magazine. He seems obsessed with sex. He leers and makes crude remarks all day long. It's like his mind has no room for anything but sex. Sometimes in the morning, when I wake up, he'll be standing by my bunk leering down at me. Sometimes, I wake up because he is touching me intimately, and I scream. He just laughs like a hyena as though he were the funniest man alive.

Coming on this boat was the worst mistake of my life.

After I read the letter I looked at Edna Quincy, perplexed. "Not very flattering of your husband," I said.

She tightened her lips and turned her head once. "He thought it was funny," she said, deflated. "That's the kind of person he was."

It only went to show that sometimes the people you wish would fall overboard sometimes do. She was willing to pay me to see if anyone helped him take the dive, so his character was neither hither nor yon.

So I asked Mrs. Quincy the question. "How much can you afford?"

I was pleasantly surprised. She was no Harold Mattlock, of course—but no Malvin Stark either. That's the real name of yours truly in his plain-wrapper mutation.

I had thought she didn't have a pot to cook in. But, she had a respectable trust fund which threw her a nice piece of the egg and the nest it lay in. So I magnanimously agreed to take installment payments that would total two-hundred thousand dollars including my expenses, if I lived that long. If I didn't produce, I would be stuck with the (not inconsiderable) expenses. It is not a contract I should be bragging about.

I did think of all the pros (two) and the countless cons, but what finally sold me was not my daughter Felicity, nor Edna Quincy—but those five ship shapely bodies on the coffee table.

When I got back home to Torrance, California, my distaff Tyrannosaurus Rex Wemple Stark was in the garage blowing glass. And no one was better constructed for that endeavor. But she was spending so much time in the garage she was starting to look like a motor vehicle—a Sherman tank.

Torrance is a town made up largely of working stiffs living in tract houses. I am such a working person, my wife Tyranny Rex is just a stiff.

It is a flat land in the shadow of the Palos Verdes Peninsula where my exalted father-in-law would hang his hat, if he had the sense to wear one. It would go a long way toward hiding his dandruff. Palos Verdes is where the swells live. That swell Elbert A. Wemple holds (as in both hands tightening around my throat) the mortgage on the house, which in twenty-some years I have paid down a few, precious few, dollars. At an interest rate that would land him an upper berth in the slammer were the authorities to come upon constructive notice of same.

Tyranny Rex and I are flatlanders, as were our

children in their turn. Elbert Daddybucks is a mountain king. He is a guy who feels it is his lot in life to be elevated over all others.

But I take heart that those of us on the flatland are less likely to roll off.

My first order of business on beginning any case was to get clear of my omnipotent wife and her insufferable father—my boss, the august Elbert August Wemple, sole proprietor of Elbert A. Wemple and Ass., Realtors—E.A. himself is the embodiment of the abbreviation for Associates.

While awaiting the surfacing of the Sherman tank from the garage, I went out back to glory in my palm and cycad collection. There was nothing so conducive to my well-being than a slow stroll among my beloved plants. Some people have dogs and cats for companions, I prefer plants—they live longer, are quieter, take less cleanup and are even more loyal than the four-legged creatures. I started my collection of rare cycads rather modestly with tiny twenty-five dollar plants that might grow into something you could see in my lifetime. But when I had my first windfall in the P.I. biz, I bought some substantial stuff, like an *Encephalartos latifrons* in a one-gallon pot—the whole thing about thirty inches tall—for two thousand dollars. Some I paid more for or less, but any way you sliced it, you didn't cover a lot of ground for the money.

My latest catch was an *Encephalartos poggei*, for the same price. It has two leaves and if my math is correct, that's a thousand dollars a leaf. That will give you some idea of the excitement I get on seeing a new leaf pop out of the caudex—that roundish base of the plant that looks something like a closed-shop pine cone. The size of that caudex along with the rarity of the plant determines its price. If precision is called for, the size of the caudex is given in inches of diameter and height out of the ground. The length and number of leaves seems immaterial as the size of the caudex determines the potential of the plant.

If less precision is acceptable, the plant size is communicated by comparison—it is like a ping-pong ball, lime, lemon, softball, grapefruit, football, volleyball or basketball.

To make it easy on the seller, a hundred dollars an inch of diameter is often used as a guideline for many *Encephalartos*—the most sought after of the eleven genera of cycads. This generalizing of price to size makes it easier on the seller than the buyer. Why a hundred dollars an inch? Why not ten dollars? No other plants in the world command such a price with such little potential for growth. And there is perhaps no other sucker in the world like an excited *Encephalartos* buyer. His roundish head is also reminscent of that closed up pine cone, but head size has no relation to rationality where purchase prices are concerned. I was well aware I often paid too much for those strange plants, but you have to realize how circumscribed my life was between Tyranny Rex and Daddydandruff. The windfalls from my P.I. successes have given me something to live for—my palm and cycad garden.

My triangle palms—planted in a triangle, of course—were doing well. They were up to my eyeballs after seven or eight years. The queens and kings were overhead, and I was beginning to get a slight jungley feeling out behind my house. I bought the palms for about twenty-five bucks a piece.

The downside of leaving home for my investigating enterprise was leaving my palms and cycads. But I always took along pictures of my garden in its latest state, like one would take remembrances of a loved one.

If I left the garden in Tyranny's care I'm afraid I'd return to a plant cemetery, so I hire a neighbor girl to water. She gets a kick out of the responsibility and does a conscientious job.

Tyranny Rex doesn't know a cycad from Shinola.

From time to time people have asked me what my goal is with my garden, or what percent complete it is. I don't have any idea. But my small lot was getting to the point of being stuffed to capacity. As the palms grew and the fronds touched fronds from other plants and hit me in the face when I passed, I began to realize I was running out of space. So with my largest investigating largess I bought the house next door and began planting that. I rented out the house, marking my entry into the landlord biz. I wasn't so naive that I thought Daddybucks Wemple would welcome this nascent flapping of my wings but would rather view it as a sinister plot to put him out of business. The fact that he had me about 800 living units to one wouldn't cube any ice with him.

So I could do no less than keep the transaction from both Wemples *pere et fille*. Tyranny didn't notice anything different. Her mind was on blowing glass. If anything she might have wondered why I had suddenly become so friendly with the new neighbors. If she thought it strange that the neighbors had suddenly taken an interest in palms and cycads—to the tune of replanting the yard exclusively with these plants, she didn't mention it.

As I commune with my palms and cycads, my mind clears of the detritus of everyday existence with the eccentric Wemples. I can concentrate on my cases. In this case, a case of breaking down a liar in a sniveling confession. It wasn't going to be any harder because the five-member crew was made up of gorgeous young women. But it wouldn't be any easier, either.

Then, surprises of surprises, Tyranny Rex made a rare appearance in the garden. I could feel the earth shake because Tyranny was such a presence you thought the earth was quaking at her step. "There you are," she said, as though my whereabouts were of the slightest interest to her.

"Malvin! What are you going to *do* with all these plants? I can hardly move out here anymore."

This charming utterance on her part begged a certain response like "Move? Have you been in the house lately? It is so full of your ridiculous glass figurines even the flies have trouble moving."

Instead, I muttered, "Sorry." That's me—Malvin Stark. Or that's me as I used to be before I backed into this private eye enterprise. A wimp I was. Still am at home. But on the road as Gil Yates, the high-priced contingency investigator, smoke my watch, or however that saying goes.

Before Tyranny opened her mouth again, I speculated on what was going to come out of it. Would it be, "I have a meeting to go to. You'll have to get your own dinner," or would it be some random criticism of my person or being?

But, no, she drew in a breath that puffed her up like the Hindenburg before it exploded. If only *she* would explode, mankind might be better served.

"Remember, this is my big art fair week in Santa Barbara and I'm behind, so there won't be much for dinner."

I nodded. I had become adroit at the subservient nod. Humble pie with the Wemples always stood me in good stead. She twirled on her substantial heels causing my *Dypsis lucubensis* fronds to flap in her wake as she marched, secure in the completion of her duty, back to her lifeblood staples, the urinating farm boy and the "all new" defecating cow.

It gave me an inspiration. As soon as she was gone out the door, I would leave her a note and follow. My note would say I was going to visit our daughter Felicity in Hawaii where she was doing her best to defeat the educational system at the University of Hawaii—as she had in her time done at various other institutions of higher learning.

Felicity's higher education credentials include El Camino Junior College, Santa Barbara City College, Arizona State, San Diego State, Long Beach State and now the University of Hawaii. I may have forgotten a few in there. Places she spent less than a semester got a little hazy. Her educational interests seemed to begin and end with men in sunny climes. In between she toyed with acting classes and anything else she thought would make her a beloved movie star. That, apparently, is no easy task in the college and university system.

I won't say Felicity was importuning the educational system, neither was she the perpetual student in pursuit of never ending learning. She was rather a person with a penchant for putting off the rest of her life by sticking herself in a safe groove insulated and isolated from reality. She was not unlike her mother, Tyrannosaurus Rex, in that regard.

I would call the office late that night, on my way to the airport and leave a message for Elbert A. Wemple, Ass., Realtor—with just enough mystery about my whereabouts to drive him up the fence. The further I got from Daddy Pimple the easier he was to take.

When I heard the door to the garage close and I knew Tyranny Rex was safely in her haven of glass trinkets which she always managed to sell under cost—when she managed to sell them at all—I took the five pictures of the shapely ship crew and studied them.

Perhaps, I thought, if I look at these pictures long enough, and hard enough, and with enough single-minded concentration, I will gain some insight into the workings of their minds, into the secrets of each in order to divine the murderer.

And if the pictures revealed none of that, just looking at those five astonishing beauties would be reward enough. There was simply no gainsaying one thing: Old Les Quincy sure knew how to pick 'em. I don't know if any of those knockouts could sail a boat to save their lives, but they sure would liven the bleak ocean scenery while the boat was floundering in the storm.

And if I floundered on the job? I will have had enough sensual inspiration to last a lifetime.

Well...maybe...

I was off to Honolulu feeling as I always did when obliged to fly—like a kamikaze pilot. Like this was the last glorious mission for God and country.

The swashbuckling Gil Yates would never admit to any fears—flying not withstanding.

But if you will think objectively for a minute—I'm no physicist, but you load a thing that weighs tons and tons empty, load it, say, with another fifty thousand pounds or so—people, bags and stuff—and how do you expect it to stay up? Air will hold it up? Where is the logic?

Take a pencil—weighing not much more than a fly—and push it off a table. Does air hold it up?

Or make a paper airplane and toss it across the room. What happens?

There is a never-ending amazement in the number of people who march in lock step onto an airplane like sheep to the slaughter—looking just as blasé as if they were crossing a country road.

Malvin Stark simply does not fly—for all the aforementioned reasons. But, when I became Gil Yates there were certain macho expectations which I was obliged to fulfill. Flying was one of them.

So, I took a cab to the Los Angeles International Airport, whose abbreviation is LAX. Does that build any confidence when they *admit* the operation is lax? In capital letters?

It was the pictures of the stunning sailors that saved me from apoplexy in the airport. I took them out and stared at them one by one, so intently I blocked out all else, except, of course, the nagging thought that this was probably my last day on earth.

What did you do when all you had to go on was pictures and an address at the time of the accident? I didn't get the easy cases. Easy cases were for the nickel and dimers, so much a day plus expenses. My contingency racket produced higher end fees, but it carried higher risks.

I always had a yen to fly first class. I had visions of Tyranny Rex and her insufferable father seeing the roster of crash victims with Gil Yates among the select first-class passengers. Then I realized they wouldn't even know who Gil Yates was. They know zip about my other life.

I imagine flying coach would be quite exciting if you were a worm. Oodles of legroom. I don't know who designs the space they allot for the beleaguered passengers, but it seems to shrink at every turn—even from the start of the flight to the finish. Someday, I plan to write a letter to the president of the airline and suggest they could squeeze more passengers in if they laid them horizontally, floor to ceiling. It might be inconvenient for feeding and going to the bathroom, but the food they serve would serve humanity better were it not served—and eliminating food or drink would cut down on the need to eliminate, and several of those palatial baths could be eliminated, making room for even more paid fares.

The pictures on my lap were in color. The young buck to my left was going to need a chiropractor when we landed, he was twisting his neck so hard to look at them. If I had been a social animal I may have invited his attention. Instead I did contortions of my own to keep him from seeing my private harem.

The pictures had a sameness about them, yet they were all different. I could see how Les Quincy picked his crew. They all looked fit, strong and knock-down-dead beautiful. Three were in minimal bikinis. One was nude—but an arty shot more suggestive than revealing. One was in shorts with a halter top but no imagination was required to see her dimensions were generous. I wondered if all the entrants sent pictures of themselves in skimpies, or just the successful ones.

The name Mrs. Quincy had penned on the back of the picture of the redhead with the shorts and halter—which qualified her as the most dressed of the bunch—was Ruth, the letter writer. She looked the most out of place in this crowd, not only because she was overdressed, but her expression didn't lend itself to this sexy exploit.

The name on the back of the nude was Sooshe. I thought that must have been a nickname. She was a thin, dirty blond. Her expression was wistful, and it made me think she needed the job more than the others.

The others were brunette Elizabeth, Prudence, raven haired, and Kay, brassy blond. Kay looked oldest and most able to handle herself. Elizabeth was exhibiting a bravado I wasn't convinced she had, and Prudence had a tilt to her head that suggested she wanted to be taken seriously and she was no pushover.

I speculated on their strong points, as well as their flaws without reaching any conclusions.

The photo of Les Quincy was predictable. Thin, tanned, muscular, his shirt off, his expansive, sensuous chest—sawed off jeans, showing, as they say, buns of steel. He was hoisting the jib or whatever you called that sail. His face was strong and virile, but the features were soft and boyish, like the schoolyard bully who ruled by intimidation. I could imagine Les appealing to women who wanted to mother him and to be dominated at the same time. He looked like a man who was more than a little stuck on himself—an authoritarian captain.

He may have been wrong about one of his crew. Fatally wrong.

4

If anyone could hold a hand-dipped candle to avaricious airlines for stacking the bodies, it was the main drag in Honolulu. One highrise cheek by dewlaps with the next. Dewlaps has always been one of my favorite words. So descriptive; it has so much flair and panache. I use it at the least opportunity. These clunky highrises were all colors, shapes and sizes, most of them industrial ugly. But with weather like that, the received wisdom must be, who cares about architecture?

The sun was up, giving so many pasty bodies a shot at skin cancer. It seemed impossible to avoid some character from South Dakota who underestimated the power of old sol and resultantly looked like a recently boiled lobster. On the ocean side of the street, highrises were planted in the sand. They grew so tall it seemed they had been watered and fertilized by the sewer systems of the buildings themselves. A kind of reverse osmosis, I supposed.

What is man but fertilizer? Women are a different kettle of gefiltefish altogether. Getting a handle on five women was my challenge. Six if you counted my daughter.

Felicity likes two things from her parents: her space and her subsistence checks. I am happy to give her the former—her grandfather the latter.

That's the way Daddy Pimple thinks. He couldn't conceive of paying me a living wage so I could pay my daughter's college expenses. Maybe for Felicity that's a good thing because I don't think I'd feed Felicity's college habit with quite so much abandon as Elbert A. Wemple...Ass. does.

It is a real treat to watch Felicity manipulate old man Wemple. She treats his counterfeit pearls of wisdom as magnum discoveries of epic proportions—he rambles, she giggles and makes big, wide eyes. He eats it up while she wraps him around her little finger. He writes her another check for another year of boondoggling, and she giggles her gratitude.

When I think what I have to do to get a $25 toilet bowl for an apartment to replace a cracked one, I get the giggles too.

Felicity doesn't like us to call her at school. She says it breaks her concentration. She prefers, she says, to call us. When she needs money. So it was not without some trepidation that I dialed her number after landing with all my limbs intact at the Honolulu airport.

Some guy answered. He sounded like his mind was elsewhere, if that were not too generous an assessment. He was at pains to tell me she was in the library, and I must confess my first thought was what in the world would she be doing in the library? In my day, libraries held books, and I could think of nothing further from her interests.

"Will you tell her, please, her father called. I'm in town and I would consider it a rare privilege to see her." I left the phone number of the hotel where I would be staying.

"Cool," was all he said before he hung up.

I found a hotel room from which the ocean was not visible. I didn't want any distractions—like a major drain on my bank account. It was not a room that was so commodious I never wanted to leave it. So I got right to work and headed for the local cops.

I wish all police forces were as friendly and accommodating as the Honolulu department.

Lt. Makai was by birth and girth all Hawaiian. I was never once made to feel like the impostor I was.

He overflowed the chair behind his desk. I sat comfortably facing him.

"Sure I remember the case," he said. "Very strange."

"Anything else you would have done if you had more time or resources to devote to it?"

He shook his head and his dewlaps jiggled like soundwaves. "What could you do? Dredge the Pacific Ocean for a body?" There was no doubt in his tone about his feel for the futility of that. "No telling what a bunch of sharks could do with a bloody body..." he snapped his fingers. "Pfft."

"Think the sharks got him?" I asked.

"I imagine," he said. "So even if we spent six months in the area and pulled up a skeleton, it wouldn't tell us anything about the cause of death."

He had a breadfruit body and sat looking at me over a myriad of chins, but there was a smile on his round face that put me at ease.

"Did you get to question all the crew?"

He nodded. "Some crew," he said, smiling at the memory like a man floating to heaven. "We detained them." He lifted both hands on the end of hamhock arms. "Nothing."

"What were their stories?"

"All asleep," he said, his mouth barely moving beneath a cocked eye.

"Believe it?"

He shrugged. "Had some suspicions..." One hand came up this time. Energy conservation. "One of those things—unless one of them felt like confessing, we really had nothing. No body, no motive—"

"No motive?"

"Not so's any of them would admit to anything. Hardest case you can imagine—guy disappears out in the ocean. Survivors claim not to know anything. I didn't like the smell of it, but—"

"Any specific suspicions?"

"Nah—didn't go that deep. They all held pretty good that they were sound asleep—heavy work, hot sun, exhausted, slept soundly—the whole bit."

"Didn't buy it?"

"Nah, Not really. The skipper...what was his name?"

"Quincy."

"Yeah. He was in great shape. Nobody had any reason he might have committed suicide. He was a seasoned sailor so it's unlikely he would have fallen overboard. Besides, he was an excellent swimmer."

"Beloved by his troops?" I added with a question.

He pursed his ample lips. "That's a little more problematic. When I read between the lines, I wasn't so sure."

"Specifics?"

"Nothing I could put my finger on. I don't think he was beloved around here. One of the crew claimed she and the captain were to be married, but of course he had a wife on the mainland. Seems a strange boatload of people, but I got the impression most of them had a good idea of what they were getting into. Except one may be questionable."

"Who was that?"

"A religio—don't remember her name. Something biblical, I think." He raised an eyebrow. "Not exactly the gig you'd expect would attract one of a holy bent."

"Could I look at the boat?" I asked.

He hoisted his massive shoulders. "Get your scuba diving gear."

"Sank?"

"Yeah."

"Accident?"

"Hah."

"Who sank it?"

The shoulders lifted again. "Strange business," he said.

"How so?"

"Boat blew up before anyone reported Les missing. Only way we heard about the case was the insurance claim. They had to file a police report to make their claim on the insurance."

"Anybody see it happen?"

"Old guy on the pier. Big explosion. Two boats go out and one comes back."

"No one went down with it?"

"Not that we know."

"Look for it?"

"Not too hard. Insurance problem. No one filed a criminal complaint."

"Ideas?"

"Les Quincy's mother got the pay off. Not likely she was complicit in her own son's death. A Christian woman," he said, as though that explained her innocence. I wasn't so sure.

"Remember her name?"

"It's in the file."

"Why do you think there was no police report of Les's disappearance?"

He lifted his leaden shoulders. "Maybe nobody missed him—or cared."

"His mother?"

His head bobbed.

"Coverup? Foul Play?"

He nodded again. "Just couldn't get the goods," he said. "Short of confession and corroboration, there isn't much to hang a case on."

"Any theories?" I asked.

He smiled and looked over my head. "Lots of theories," he said.

"Such as?"

"The boy was in trouble. Used this as a gimmick to disappear."

"Why sink the boat?"

"Couple ideas. Maybe there was something incriminating. Two, maybe Mom preferred the money to the boat."

"You didn't want to arrest the girls for not reporting the crime?"

He shrugged. "Could have." Then he shook his head. "A no winner. Imagine going to a jury on this island with the establishment against those five beauties. With the victim a reprobate like Les Quincy." His head swivelled again. "You wouldn't even need to put on a defense. The district attorney wouldn't touch it with a ten-foot pole."

"Anything else?"

He thought a moment. "Not really. You want to see the file?"

"I'd be grateful," I said.

He pushed himself up from his desk, not an easy operation, and led me down the hall into a cavernous room filled with file cabinets. He found the applicable repository, opened the drawer and withdrew a folder less than an inch thick.

"Here it is," he said, handing it to me, "not much, I'm afraid."

He let me take the file to the copy machine. "Dupe anything you want," he said. "You can hand it in at the desk when you leave."

Island casual.

We shook hands, and he hauled himself out of the cavern.

I glanced at the file contents. The names and addresses were all there. Even mug shots taken, I took it, by the cops. They all seemed to have been dressed for the photo session.

There was little excitement in the text of the report. Every sailor claimed she was sound asleep. No frills, no embellishments, no leads.

Except the names, addresses and phone numbers.

But they were almost a year old.

I hit a couple of waterfront bars around the marina before I landed a bartender who remembered Les Quincy.

The contrast between the inside of the Ahoy Mate and the outside of Honolulu marina couldn't have been more stark. Bright and sunny outside, movie-house dark inside. Perhaps not coincidental. A person coming from the outside in needs a few moments to adjust his eyes to the darkness. So they stand there looking like a proverbial doe in the headlights and the barkeep can get a quick but usually reliable fix on the new sucker.

I don't suppose it took him more than a nanosecond to recognize me as a land lubber. When my pupils adjusted, I saw a squat bartender with early attempts at a dirty blond beard. He had his right hand on the waistband of his pants (no belt) and he pulled them up with a jerking punctuation motion.

I made my way to the bar, sans seeing-eye dog.

Bars seem to have personalities of their own. But then so do junkyards. I am about as familiar with one as the other. And I am seeing some similarities between the two.

In one the bottles are full, in the other, empty. The furniture is often in a similar state of repair. Moreover there are many other crossovers in decor from fishnets and buoys to rusty anchors and boat parts. Down there at the waterfront where the sailors put in for shore leave the ambiance is heavy on the nautical. Reminds them of their dreary lives at sail, I suppose. Makes them drink more. If they had been my places, I would have thrown in some potted palm trees. Not cycads, of course, too valuable, too portable.

Not too much thought went into naming this particular place the Ahoy Mate. With so many bars to choose from, a catchy name would seem prudent.

From what I could make out in the dark, this saloon was tilting to a sea-worthy ambiance—the exposed pipes of a battle ship, nets from a trawler, a wheel and compass from a cruise ship.

I felt like a stowaway.

I ordered a bottle of designer water and the barkeep didn't seem to mind. I focused on a plastic breast plate with "Hi, I'm Marty" painted in black letters on a gold, glittery background. When he served my two-dollar water, I noticed a nice crust of vintage dirt on the bottle.

I asked him if he knew Les Quincy of the all-girl crew fame.

"Yah, I remember Les. He'd have a few and get to talkin' 'bout his boat an' the all girl crew." Marty, the barkeeper hiked up his pants whenever he wanted to make a point. "Pretty pleased with himself, you ask me."

"Blame him?" I asked.

Marty smiled. "Can't say as I do. Wouldn't that be something?" and Marty's eyes drifted to the ceiling. I could tell he was picturing all the best aspects of being alone on the ocean with five gorgeous babes.

"He ever tell you anything about...how it was?"

"Oh, yeah," Marty said. "Couldn't shut him up sometimes. According to him, it was like a paradise—the five of them took turns. See there was only four single bunks. The cap'n, he had a double. Five girls, you do the math."

"And they all went for it?"

"'Cording to him. They didn't, he didn't hire 'em in the first place."

"What if one of them changed her mind?"

He grinned, then hiked up his pants. "She better be an awful good swimmer."

"Any theories on how he died?"

"Nah. Lot of scuttlebutt about the local establishment disapproving of his, shall we say, lifestyle, but there's nothing to go with it. He was at sea, middle of the night. No witnesses. Girls could never overpower him unless they got him unconscious first."

"How?"

"That's the hooker, of course. Drugs? Hit him on the head with a hammer when he wasn't looking? Got me."

He ever mention any of the girls by name?"

"Nah—oh, he might say she was a redhead or a blond or something. I don't remember any names."

"Kay Sagerstrom ring any bells?"

He thought for only a second before shaking his head.

"She lives here, I'm told."

"Lot of people do," he allowed.

"Ever tell you he was going to marry one of 'em?"

"He did say something about one of 'em getting pregnant. No talk of marriage though."

"Which one? Give you anything to go on? Name, hometown, hair color?"

He shook his head. "Old Les was pretty much a braggart. Sometimes I got the idea he didn't even know their names. Or he made up his own names. Probably just said 'Hey, you,' when he wanted to call 'em." He paused for a special thought or two. "Kinda like a dog or something."

"Think he could have done himself in?"

"Hah! not that one. Too in love with himself." Marty hiked up his pants. "We don't kill our best friends." Marty the bartender was a good Joe.

I thought it was a long shot, but I consulted the phonebook outside the men's room in back. Miracle of miracles, Kay was listed with an address.

I considered calling, but experience taught me surprise was the better approach to someone who might not want to talk to you.

I piled into my rental car and headed for the hills—after consulting my map—and a pretty posh address up the street from the Botanic Garden.

I was tempted to stop first at the garden to check out the palms and cycads, many of which I could not grow in Southern California. But duty was yelling and I steered the course.

The address went with a white stucco job with a balcony running the width of the second story. Red tiles on the roof. Nice, lush, tropical landscaping with some *Pritchardia* palms in front.

One look at her pad told me life had treated Kay Sagerstrom well since the unfortunate accident. I wondered if she might not have held a handsome insurance policy on skipper Quincy.

I didn't have time for subtleties, so I knocked on the front door. It was some little time before it was opened by a blond woman in a sarong of lime green with cabbage-sized silver and gold flowers and a magnolia in her hair. Her smile was of the familiar-flirtatious mien and I felt a sudden weakness in the knees.

"I'm Gil Yates," I said, and she was right there with—

"Hi, Gil—I'm Kay."

She didn't know if I was from the Jehovah's Witnesses, the Women's Christian Temperance Union or a homeless shelter, and yet she was as welcoming and friendly as all get out.

"I'm here about Les Quincy."

Her face dropped. I could see a homeless man would have been preferable.

She sighed the sigh of the helpless, trapped beyond escape. "What about him?" she said with a slight Brooklyn accent. She was like a woman caught without her makeup, though she was severely attractive without it. There was an engaging beauty about her face, but not without a tough quality that put you on notice that she could handle herself.

"His widow wants to know how he died," I said.

"Didn't she read the report?" she asked. "He was never found," she shrugged as though that closed the case.

"She thought you and your fellow crew members might shed a little light. Make it go down easier."

"Well isn't that nice? She was no wife to him while he was alive. Now all of a sudden, she's Florence Nightingale?"

"Want to talk about it?" I asked.

"Not really," she said, wearily. "I'm talked out—but I can see I'll have no rest from you..." then she brightened. "Besides," she said, with a twinkle in her eye, "you're not a bad-looking man." She turned and said facing away from me. "Come on." The sarong was loose everywhere but clung as if glued to the most magnificently sculpted gluteus maximus in memory.

I followed the waving sarong into a flower-scented sun porch that overlooked her lush backyard to the Pacific Ocean beyond.

"You seem to have liked him."

She looked out at a *Cyphophoenix elegans* palm. "I was his favorite," she said, her eyelashes going batty.

"Anybody jealous of that?"

"What do you think? Five girls, one guy? He picks me above all else? You figure."

"Anyone specific in mind?"

"Oh, they were all jealous. He favored me from the start. Even that little religious freak. She was subtle about it, but I could see she wanted him—on her own terms, of course, and he never would have gone for that, even if he was turned on by her, which he was not."

We sat on those eminently breathable rattan chairs with plum-hued tropical patterned cushions. She called it the veranda.

The garden in front of us was resplendent.

There were three *Cycas taitungensis*, booming to beat the wind ensemble. New leaves were pouring out of the cottony caudex like ash from a volcano. There was a small group of *Zamia fischeri* under a couple of *Hyophorbe verschaffeltii* as well as *lagenicaulis*, which I can't grow in Southern California.

You couldn't beat Hawaii for growing this tropical stuff. And while Kay was rambling small talk I fantasized buying a couple of acres here and growing palms I couldn't grow at home. I could be close to Felicity—for the next five years or so while she completed her sophomore year.

Palms grew faster here, too—there was a *Pritchardia martii* that left mine in the dust. It was about eight feet tall—mine two feet on tiptoes.

"We were going to be married, you know," she said, looking at me to see if I registered the desired shock.

"He wasn't married?" I hoped to sound startled.

She waved me off. "He was going to divorce her."

"When was this going to happen?"

"Soon," she put a handkerchief to her nose. "After the trip, he was getting a divorce."

"Did his wife know?"

"She knew it was over."

"Had they discussed divorce?" I didn't mean to doubt her, but that was how she took it. Her neck stiffened.

"She *knew*," she reiterated in an icy tone.

"So, what do you think happened?"

Kay looked at me a long time as if attempting to discover if she could trust me. "I was asleep," she said.

"Yes, I've heard you were all asleep. I'm just asking for speculation."

"Speculation is folly."

"Do you think *everyone* was asleep?"

"I don't know. That's what the police believed. I only know I was asleep. I'm a sound sleeper. The sun, the activity, the constant strain takes it out of you. I sleep like a log."

"Um," I intoned noncommittally. "Where were you sleeping?"

"With him," she said, without hesitation.

"For the whole trip?"

"No. We rotated. But after he decided to marry me, it was just me and him."

"Anybody else object to that?"

"The sleeping arrangements, like everything else on the ship, were up to the captain. We learned that right up front. The captain of a ship is a dictator."

"Everybody bought into that okay?" I asked.

"More or less," she said with a shrug. "When you are on the ocean, you don't have a lot of options."

"You knew the arrangements in advance."

"We did."

"And all the women agreed to, ah, (I hoped I wasn't blushing) taking turns like that?"

"It wasn't compulsory. Our religious nut resisted, but Les had no trouble filling her slot. Sometimes, Les didn't replace her, so the other four bunks were full and she could sleep with him in his commodious double bed, or alone on the floor."

"She chose the floor?"

She nodded slowly. "That's my understanding, but as I said, I'm a sound sleeper."

I was beginning to wonder how sound a sleeper anyone could be with six people on a thirty-five foot boat. "Now, Kay—I'm sure you have thought about this… accident, since it happened. Are you convinced it *was* an accident?"

"Convinced? I'm not *convinced* of anything."

"Any suspicions?"

"Hey, I've had suspicions. I just have nothing to back them up."

"What are they? Or should I say, whom do you suspect?"

She took a deep breath—"Look, we were all interviewed by the Honolulu police. Nobody saw anything. I mean, that was unanimous. Yet, think about it. How could it be? Nothing is going to convince me Les Quincy just dove over the side of the boat and drowned."

"Could he have hit his head on a railing or on the sail or something and fallen overboard?"

"That's about as likely as being struck by lightning when there was no lightning."

"Any of the women dislike him?"

"Hah! Sure, we all had reasons to be put out with Les. He could be very trying at times and you're getting that from his fiancée."

"What were some of the gripes?"

"How much time have you got?"

"Lots."

"Ruth was a prude. I myself love the physical aspect of a relationship. Ruth was holier than the whole boatload of us. She resented his hedonism. But she was a babe in the woods. I was married, had two kids, was looking for relief from my suffocating union—Ruth was looking for a lark."

"Did all the others accept this rotation of bed partners?"

"In varying degrees. At different times. As I said, he couldn't make it compulsory. Only Ruth refused. Les Quincy was very good in that department."

"Did you all get along?"

"Five women, one man? You kidding?"

"Any physical fights?"

"No."

"Words?"

"Now and then."

"With the skipper?"

"Oh, those close quarters. You are bound to have some disagreements."

"Like?"

"Oh, it's been almost a year. I can't remember specifics. Nothing worth killing over."

"What can you tell me about the other women?"

"Oh, it was quite an assortment, we had the Jesus freak, Ruth, we had the perpetual hippie—Sooshe, what a name, huh? Like raw fish!"

"He like her?"

"He liked me best."

How could you follow that? I didn't have to; she went on under her own hot air. "Then there was that southern bitch—excuse me, that's belle, isn't it? Southern belle. Prudence her name was, if you can believe it. All I could think of was, it wouldn't be prudent, and she wasn't. Elizabeth was a tanned California girl—in great shape. I always wondered if she was strong enough to take Les out. Of the whole crew, if strength were the criteria, Elizabeth took the ribbon."

"What was her background?"

"Don't know. Had the notion she was running from the law, but it was sketchy. But I guess we were all running from something. I from my suffocating marriage, others from loneliness, boredom, persecution—you name it—real or imagined."

I worked up the courage to leave her with the question that was bugging me. "Did you win this great house in the lottery—or a lucky divorce?"

She laughed. "It's not mine. I live here with my friend, the Admiral. He's a dear—retired now, but I'm in love for the first time." She referred to him as the Admiral, as though he were a poop deck. She glanced at her watch, then jumped up. "Goodness, I'm late. I'm meeting him for cocktails, will you excuse me?" and she showed me hastily to the door.

Felicity, my darling daughter, did not deign to return my phone calls. She was not a child who suffered her parents gladly. It was a stance I could concede where her mother was concerned, but not her dear old dad.

The sundry fellows who answered the phone all had the lingo down pat. “Felicity,” they said, “is at the library studying.” If she had spent half the time studying they said she did, she would be well on her way to a Ph.D. instead of mired as she was in her Sophomore year.

Many professions had these dodges: realtors were showing property, lawyers in court, scientists in the lab, doctors at the hospital.

“Students” were in the library.

I always thought Honolulu would be a nice place to live if you happened to be a humpback whale. Sun, surf, sand, glitz, and pretty people who looked like they spent too much time in a tanning salon on rainy days.

My own Felicity sported a respectable tan, which

I'd no doubt she picked up in the library.

I decided to sneak up on her. The library was not the first place I looked. It was in her apartment, early the next morning. So early, I guessed her eyes would not yet be open.

I guessed correctly.

Daddy Pimple had sported Felicity to pretty posh digs close enough to the university so she could get there on foot, minimizing the excuses for cutting classes.

Felicity was a child who had honed hedonism to a fine art. Within her means, or I should say, within the endurance of Daddy Dandruff and the indulgences of his pocketbook, which all came down to the creativity of Felicity's appeals. I had the feeling he saw through Felicity's clever cadging, but he was so amused by her creativity that he wrote the check. He was a sucker for a granddaughter but a miser with his son-in-law. His only son-in-law I might add, because Dorcas was an only child, and if you saw Dorcas a.k.a. Tyrannosaurus Rex, you wouldn't have to ask why.

Felicity's apartment was upstairs on a multi-unit conglomeration. There was a row of blue doors that stood out from the white stucco-like whale teeth. I knocked on Felicity's door several times before rousing her.

I heard her groggy voice through the door.

"Who is it?"

I debated telling her I was from the lottery and she'd won, because I was not entirely sanguine if I said I was her father, she would open the door.

Gil Yates was out. While she didn't know the name, my alter ego being unknown to my family, I couldn't use that *nom de plume.*

"An old friend," I said, with only the slightest attempt made to disguise my voice. She went for it—owing, I suppose, to her unfamiliarity with her father's voice.

The door opened a crack and I saw my only daughter in a skimpy nightgown peer at me and register in the same split second the horror of recognition.

"Oh, Pops," she said, closing the door. "Just a minute," her voice of panic came through the door. "I have to straighten up...get decent."

Get decent, I thought. How decent would she have had to get if it hadn't been her father, who had, whether she knew it or not, changed quite a few of her diapers. Tyranny Rex was not what you'd call a totally engaged mother, her mind being on loftier things like blowing glass.

The door bolted open and a young man, disheveled and disturbed, bolted out and tore down the balcony walkway to disappear down the steps.

It is unfair to make snap judgments, but I pegged him for a gas pump jockey (self-service gas stations making that a simpler task) or to give him the benefit of the doubt, an auto mechanic. I just felt he would have been connected with automobiles somehow—or motorcycles. I was just betting myself he was some kind of monkey with a surefit of grease under his fingernails when I heard the unmistakable roar of the Harley below, the great booming sound crescendoing as he whisked by, leaving in its wake the reverberation and smell of exhaust that bystanders to those unique machines had come to love.

It wasn't long after (perhaps ten minutes) that

the door opened and there was my daughter forcing a grin. "Come on in, Pops." She turned and seemed to be sucked up by her living room. I followed. "Ought to call first," she said. "I have a hectic day."

"Call? I called a half-dozen times," I said.

She didn't argue.

"I suppose it will be less hectic now that the motorcycle jockey is clear of the place."

"Oh, that was my study partner."

"Got an early start, didn't you?"

"Yeah, well, like I say this day is real crazy. So, what can I do for you?" She was treating me like a salesman who had intruded on a pleasant dream.

"A social call," I said.

"Geez," she said. "Couldn't be a worse time. I don't have much to offer you—some instant coffee?"

I just looked at her. My own daughter didn't realize her father didn't drink coffee.

Felicity favored her mother, which is to say we never had to bear the agony of anorexia nervosa. She definitely wasn't fat in the perjorative sense of the word, but next to her ballet-dancing brother she was somewhat rotund.

She had an engaging face, if you were attuned to short engagements and a relaxed manner about her which belied her incessant talk about how hectic things were.

It wasn't unusual to be talking to her and have the sense she was sleeping with her eyes open.

It crossed my mind that I shouldn't sit in her living room without asking. My relationship to my daughter was like old acquaintances who, while not wishing to renew the old relationship exactly, were more or less curious about how the other had filled the time since the last, probably distant, meeting.

I admit I was curious about Felicity, though I had important doubts she was curious about me. We were only a generation apart though sometimes it seemed like a millennium.

Her place was a repository for everything she had ever taken a fancy to. She was her mother's daughter all right. Stuffed animals, clothing, pictures of friends—one of her brother, none of her parents—*de rigueur* school books (she was adroit at embracing the trappings of the student), nascent collections of boxes, jewelry, soap ends, string, rubber bands, makeup, combs, scarves, shoes. There was a large poster picture on the living room wall of Brad Pitt, topless. She even kept some glass figurines her mother had sent her. A ballerina, a little boy reading a book, a boy and girl holding hands (no doubt meant to represent Felicity and her brother August. Charming.) and the ubiquitous urinating boy who enjoyed an honored position in her glass menagerie.

They sat like toy soldiers on a coffee table in front of a tattered couch, mingling freely with notebooks, coffee cups, candy wrappers and a half-eaten tuna-salad sandwich which several flies seemed to be enjoying.

Either the defecating cow, one of Tyranny's latest concoctions, had not made it to Hawaii, or Felicity had the good taste to throw it out. It must have been the former for the latter stretched credulity to its popping point. Felicity never threw anything out.

I took the bull by the teeth and began assuming the motions of a sitting posture when I heard Felicity say, "Oh, don't sit down. Take me someplace for breakfast."

"All right," I said slowly, just remembering that Felicity turned every meeting with a parent into a feeding opportunity. She simply could not envision her mom and dad—or Mumsie and Pops as she reveled in calling us—as anything other than milk cows with swollen udders.

To complete her portrayal of a student, she slung a sloppy bookbag over her shoulder, announcing that she simply had to hit the library immediately after breakfast because this was some crazy day. Pop quizzes, papers due, exams; if she survived, it would be a miracle.

Felicity was always so careful to make me feel like an inopportune intruder.

We settled into one of those booths that had borne the imprints of decades of derrières, and Felicity let out some air as though the weight of the world had given her no options.

"No really, Pops, what brings you to the islands?"

"You."

"Me? Come on. I've never been sure you remembered my name."

"Dorcas, isn't it?" I said with a good humor of a man who knows he's been trapped.

"That's Mumsie," she said, sans smile.

"I knew it was one of you," I said. "So, how's it going?"

"Crazy," she said, "like I said. I'm up to my eyeballs in work."

Work? What a charming word to hear clear her lips. It connoted to me gainful employment, something so foreign to Felicity's experience that it had a comical ring.

She ordered the overeaters anonymous special with the announcement to the waitress and her Pops that she was famished. I opted for the oatmeal that had, according to the menu, been hammered and sawed by some Irishman, which I expected would make it extra tasty.

"Like school?" I asked, knowing full well what the answer would be, but nevertheless determined to make some small talk preparatory to the real thing.

"You mean I must like it because I spend so much time at it?" Her grin was engaging, you had to say that for her.

"Well..."

"It's okay."

I expected no more. "I heard a funny thing on the plane," I said with clever insouciance. "There was this young woman sitting next to me and she was chatty, you know the kind—"

She nodded.

"Seems she had been on a ship with a guy named Les something and he had an all-girl crew. Just this Les and five girls. You ever hear anything about that? Honolulu was his base port, she said."

"Les Quincy!" she exclaimed, fairly jumping out of her seat. "*I* interviewed with him."

"*You?*"

"Well, of course I didn't get the job—if you want to call it that. More of a joke, really. No pay—like an internship, but," she shrugged, "I thought it would be a fun experience, so what the hey. The guy was a creep."

"You sent a picture?"

"Oh, sure, I found one from my thinner days."

I was trying not to be judgmental, but I could tell by her edgy answers that my facial expressions were not as neutral as I'd hoped.

"But when he saw me, I saw his face drop right away. I guess he had plenty of applicants and he favored the skinnies, but it would have been a hoot."

"With a creep?"

"Well, there would have been five of us. Outnumber him—"

"So, if he offered you a slot, you'd have gone with him?"

"I guess," she said, tweaking her nose. "It would have been a trip. But I wasn't disappointed or surprised he didn't pick me."

"Why not?"

"Oh, his questions, his explanation of the trip—the sleeping arrangements."

"What were they?"

"Four bunks and the captain's. Five girls. Get it?"

I got it—both times. I nodded. "That appeal to you?"

"With that creep? No way!"

"So what would you have done—if you'd gotten on?"

"Worry about it later. I can take care of myself. Maybe that's why I didn't make it—"

"Think you'd have gone the whole three month trip?"

She laughed her short, waste-no-effort laugh. "That's one point he made—hard to get off midocean."

"So, what went through your mind? If you thought he was a creep, I mean—"

"I just thought it couldn't be that bad or he wouldn't be able to bring it off so many times."

"How many?"

"Told me this was his fifth time out."

"With only girls on the crew?"

Felicity nodded.

"Could you imagine anyone murdering him?"

"Heck yes. That's the first emotion he evokes. I wanted to murder him halfway into the interview," Felicity said then trailed off and added with a wistful sigh, "If only he weren't so... *sexy!*" She came back to earth and said, "Well Pops, thanks for the breakfast. Got to run—got a crazy day ahead of me."

"Yeah," I said. "Can I see you again while I'm here?"

"Call first," she said, and was gone with the wind.

Eminence grise opened the door. He wasn't happy to see me.

"Ah, is Kay, ah, Sagerstrom in?"

"Who wants to know?" Always a clever response, I thought. I didn't respond.

"She doesn't want to see you," he said trying to inject a little menace in his thin voice. "We're finished with trauma around here." He had a fine head of gray hair and from the dignity that poured from his pores, I realized I was face to face with the Poop Deck himself. In his salad days, he had been an honor student in posture. His glare let me know if I had been on his ship he'd have wiped his poop deck with *me.*

Just as I thought my ship was on its last legs, Kay popped out from behind the old salt.

"Honey, he can't hurt us," she scoffed. "Look at him—he's just trying to make a living. Come on in, slugger." I followed her back to the veranda and Poop Deck mercifully turned his battleship in full retreat.

"The Admiral is very protective of me," Kay said, taking a rattan seat and waving me into another. "I don't know where he gets the idea there's any trauma." She shrugged her shoulders with a good-natured twitch. "Just because you are engaged to be married one day and the next the groom is gone." Her eyes got misty. She seemed to focus on the *Clinostigma* palm in the far corner of their backyard. "Maybe Les did me a favor," she said softly.

"Think he could still be alive?"

She seemed to jump at the thought. "Well," she took a breath, "why not? We were all asleep. Maybe he knocked us out and took a powder. Now that I think of it, I wouldn't put it past him—no, not at all. It was the kind of joke he would have loved."

"How would that make you feel?" (I loved the feely questions.)

"I don't know. I thought I wanted to marry him in the worst way then—but if I had, I wouldn't have fallen in love with my Admiral."

"Were you convinced all the other crew members were innocent of any foul play?"

"Well," her eyes flapped, showing a generous load of eyeshadow like a flickering stoplight. "It hadn't occurred to me to question that they were all asleep."

"But now?"

"Well…I don't really have any basis for doubting…"

"But someone might have wanted him swimming with Davy Jones," I put it in nautical terms.

"There was Sooshe," she said making a face of distaste. "She was the only repeater on the crew. Was on the trip before and stayed with Les in Honolulu on the boat in between. Got pregnant. Les was fit to be tied. Told her in no uncertain terms to get rid of it. She refused. He refused to have anything to do with supporting it."

"Aren't there laws?"

"Of course there are, but I expect Les thought Sooshe didn't know. She wasn't what you'd call sophisticated."

"Dumb, was she?"

"Like a fox—but not really educated in the cruel world. Was a sheltered hippie, living off the land in California somewhere. To each his own..."

"Do you think you all could have been drugged that last night on board? Sleeping pills?"

"Hey, don't think I haven't thought of that. But we were always knocked out at the end of the day. None of us ever had any trouble sleeping."

"Who cooked that last dinner?"

She thought a moment. "I don't remember," she said. "Maybe Sooshe, but I don't know—Ruth? We took turns—"

"Any way to figure it out? Remember the order? When you did it last?"

She shook her head. "Sometimes we'd swap, so there wasn't any real order."

"Did Les ever cook?"

"Once in a while he helped. Hey, you know, I have this funny notion he was doing something the last night—drinks—dessert—something—but memory can't be trusted. One night was pretty much like next, and had I known beforehand that was going to be the last night, I might be able to remember it."

"What can you tell me about the others on the crew?"

"Phew! How much time do you have? You get

to know your fellow gals in those close quarters. Ruth was the religious nut. Fresh out of one of those down-home bible colleges, she read the Bible all the time she wasn't working. Les like to needle her. He'd say, 'Hey Ruth, whatcha reading?' She'd read out a pungent quote that shut him up. I always suspected she wasn't reading that at that particular time, but just said it to rile him—and it always worked.

"When she took the spot, she vowed to maintain 'my chaste status' was the way she put it. She almost did, but I egged her on. I told her you're missing the greatest experience in life. 'It will be more meaningful if I wait,' Ruth told me.

"'B.S.' I told her. Myself I had a fondness for sex, and I couldn't understand anyone who didn't."

"How did Les take her?"

"With a grain of salt, I'd say. When it was her turn in his bed, he'd play it coy, like he couldn't care less if she came to him or not."

"Did she?"

"I think there was softening in the ranks toward the end. Les could be awfully seductive when he wanted to, and he considered Ruth a challenge."

I made a mental note that Ruth might have had murder in her heart if he disturbed her chaste status without benefit of clergy. "Two more?" I said.

"There was that tedious Southern belle Prudence—another prize-winning name. Thought she was God's gift to mankind. She was between husbands, too, but Les didn't cotton to her the way he did to me."

"The fifth?"

"Elizabeth. Made a big thing about calling her

that. 'Lizzy rhymes with dizzy,' she said, and she was that but didn't want it talked about, I guess. Liz rhymed with Kadiz. And Betty with petty. Ditto. Her worst enemy was called Beth—I don't know—she had a lot of reasons for sticking with Elizabeth exclusively. I went along with it, but I was tempted once or twice to let go with a Dizzy Lizzy."

"Where did she come from?"

"California someplace. There was a feeling she wasn't kosher with the law."

"Why?"

"Oh, boyfriend stashed some hash at her place without her knowing it. That's her story when the cops came. The boyfriend disappeared, and she's left to take the rap."

"Believe it?"

"Nah, I always figured she was in on it some way. She didn't seem that naïve."

"If you had to pick one for the culprit—motive, ability, opportunity—who would it be?"

"Oh, geez, we were all asleep..."

"I know, that was the story. But...pick one."

"Sooshe, I guess. She was mad at his constant harping to get rid of the baby."

"Did she?"

"Don't know. Swore she wouldn't. Ruth would be a close second. He rode her something awful."

"Where were you when it happened?"

"On the way back. Probably thirty to thirty-five miles off shore. We were circling the island one last time."

"Why?"

"Good question. It was fun—Ruth was crazy to

get off. I think he was needling her."

"Did you have contact with anybody while you were on the boat?"

"We had a radio and cell phone. That close we were in contact with the islands."

"You ever hear anyone use the phone?"

"Sure—we all used it."

"Anything suspicious?"

She wrinkled her nose and shook her head.

"Were any of you experienced sailors?"

"Not really. Les told us what to do. We had other assignments—hoisting and shifting the sails, cooking, cleaning, polishing brass, oiling the teak; he kept us hopping. I had puttered around boats some, so I guess I had more experience than the other girls, but it wasn't much. Sooshe was on her second time around, but I didn't notice she was all that with it."

"Did you have night watches?"

"If there was a storm or something unusual. Ordinarily, no."

"The last night?"

"Nothing I remember."

"Everything normal, then Les Quincy just disappeared?"

She looked at me as though trying to see if I were mocking her. "That's pretty much it," she said, showing a touch of grief. I had the funny notion it did not come across as genuine as she had hoped.

"This sure is a nice place to live," I said. "Were you born here?"

"Oh no, I'm from the Bronx. Can't you tell from my accent?"

"Well, I..." I skirted that trick question. Is a

Bronx acccent something *anyone* would be proud of? "What brought you to Honolulu?"

"I was looking for my biological father," she said, showing some pain in her eyes.

"Find him?"

She nodded abstractly.

"See him?"

"Yes..."

"Often?"

"Til he died."

"Oh, I'm sorry. What did he die of?"

"Heart. He had a bad heart."

I could tell she was moved. Her usual flirty stance had given way to a funereal look. It didn't invite chit-chat, but I wanted to stay in her confidence. "How did you find him?" I asked.

She sighed when she looked at me, as if to determine if she could trust me with her confidences. She must have thought she could because she laid it all out.

"I knew I was adopted but I didn't think much of it—being a kid, I guess you have other concerns. Not till I had kids of my own—"

"Where are they?"

"With their father," she said in a flat tone. "I had to get away. Find myself. Find my roots. Motherhood didn't become me, I guess. When I thought about my kids and me being their mother, I realized that I didn't even know the woman who gave me life."

"You find her?"

She nodded. "Took just over four years. I'm thirty-eight now—I was about thirty-three when I started looking for her. She was okay. Had another family. Told me she was sixteen when I was born. The father was seventeen. Went into the Navy soon after to get away from her. Too young for committment—not that much in love, I guess. Duty?" She shrugged.

"So how did you find your father?"

"It wasn't easy. She had only his name and the fact he joined the Navy. I did a lot of research and leg-work. I became obsessed with finding him. My mother was just a dowdy old woman. I mean she was, like, fifty-three when I found her, but she had a lot of miles on her. If I was looking for glamour, I was looking in the wrong place. By this time I had idealized what my father would be."

"How were your adoptive parents?"

"Yeah, okay. Normal I guess—nothing spectacular, but nothing awful either. Plodders. My real dad on the other hand, I visualized as this dashing admiral of the fleet. I'd run to him like I was a kid, jumping into his arms and he would scoop me up like a feather pillow."

"Did he?"

"Well, no, not exactly. He was glad to see me. I guess I was exhausted by the chase." She let go of a short, ironic laugh. "Besides, I was too big by then to be scooped up. He was frail—bald—with a little pot belly that shook when he laughed—well, you know. But I was swept off my feet, anyway. I don't know why I thought so much of coming from his seed. I never thought of my husband that way. Not with our two kids. But all those years I was looking for my mom, I was really looking for him. And when I found mom, I was a little disappointed. That only intensified my feelings about my dad. I visualized him as something special, and when I saw him at last, I realized no one would think he was anything special, but *I* did."

"Must have been broken up when he died."

Her eyes started to tear. "That's an understatement," she said.

"When did it happen?"

"Been a year and a half now."

"Before your trip with Les?"

"Yeah. One of the reasons I went. To forget..."

"Did you succeed?"

"Nah. I'll never forget. Best I could hope for was momentary diversions. Guess I got that."

"How did you meet the Admiral?"

"This's how. He was one of the contacts I had when I was looking for Stanley—that's my father's name—Stanley Hatborough. Turned out Stanley was a Navy Captain—worked his way up through the ranks in thirty years. My Admiral was his best friend. And we just clicked. After the episode with Les and the boat, we renewed acquaintences and, well, here I am."

The Admiral entered to claim some pressing engagement and we said goodbye. I had a strong premonition we would meet again.

Stanley Hatborough, I thought as I left. Why does that name mean something to me?

What did it mean?

Preparatory to my flight off the island, I called my daughter Felicity "Call First" Stark. A new voice answered. He said she was guess where?

"The library."

I said I was calling to say goodbye...he said he would give her the message.

Less than even money was my take on that.

Interviewing Prudence would be a delicate situation. She was at the other end of the United States in Tennessee, according to my information, but what if I had been misinformed? That was a long schlepp to come up with empty fingers.

I suppose I should have saved Prudence for last, but the weekend was ahead of me and since I was working around my father-in-law/employer, that sack of lard, and my charming wife Tyranny Rex, it seemed a show bet to catch her first. My last address for Ruth was Baton Rouge, Louisiana. I'd pick her up on the same trip as Prudence. The others were in Southern California, more or less.

From the Honolulu airport I called the number

and asked for Prudence. A man answered and with strong vocal bona fides of the southern sections, demanded to know who was calling.

"This is Al Wimple," I said, trying to disguise my voice, without doing much of a job of it.

"What do you want?" He wasn't letting me off easy.

"I want to talk to Prudence Cole," I said imperiously.

"About what?"

"I'm afraid that is something I can only discuss with her. If she wants to tell you..." I let it trail off. I'd said enough.

"You are an impertinent whipper snapper," he said.

"Don't mean to be. Just doing my job. Believe me when I say it would be to her advantage to talk to me."

"She's out."

"When will she be back?"

"Don't know."

"What's the best time to talk to her? I'm in Hawaii so we have a six-hour difference—say tomorrow—the next day?"

"Don't know. How did you get this number?"

"From an insurance policy," I said, and heard him gulp. "I'll call again," I said, then hung up before he could react.

The pigeon was on the roost. I got on the plane with my shotgun, figuratively speaking.

Armed with Prudence's address from the police file and some fake confidence in the airborne division of the American economy, I made my way to Nashville,

Tennessee, a fine old southern town. From there in my rented compact car southwest to the hills and vales of a very pretty state. Lots of green trees fringed with a pale-blue sky. It was so beautiful I wondered why more people didn't live here. Nothing to do, I guessed.

It was a soothing drive, through this no-man's land. I had a hunch everybody was known for miles around and I thought it would be to my benefit to know a little more about Prudence and that nice man who'd answered the phone.

I stopped for gas at a lonely gas station dwarfed by tomorrow's wood pulp, hoping to find a lonely guy with a big mouth.

There was a shed that may have kept the elements off the proprietor, as long as the elements weren't too severe. The structure was reminiscent of the outhouse school of architecture. There was a chair for the boss for when things settled down from their somnambulant pace. It sat behind a counter that displayed candy bars that had once been passed over by Robert E. Lee. At the entry door a nice ice chest donated by the Coca Cola company during a particularly aggressive marketing drive stood effectively blocking access to the candy bars. The turnover in soft drinks was much greater than the candy bars. Soda was more southern. It cooled you off.

The man in charge was sitting in his chair, chewing on a corncob pipe. I tossed a thumb over my shoulder, down-homelike. "Self service?" I asked him.

He shook his head, but didn't move.

Finally he removed the pipe from his mouth. "Want gas?" he said, as though he were more interested in moving candy bars.

"I'd appreciate it," I said.

He seemed to consider several options, before nodding once to let me know he was acquiescing against his better judgment. Then he rose like Rip van Winkle from a long one and dragged himself around the Coca cola ice chest with inches to spare (owing to the fact he was spare himself).

I took a Coke from the ice chest to show him I knew what they were drinking down south, popped the cap and the stuff sprayed all over my face. He had a good laugh—an old timer in bib overalls.

I followed him to the pump (one). None of the agonizing decisions over premium or regular. In fact there was no indication on the pump what I was getting. It took him just short of forever to start the gas flowing into my rental.

"Lived here long?" I started casually.

"All my life," he said, watching the hose.

Seventy-some years I guessed, but I didn't ask. He didn't volunteer.

"Know any folks in Lucy County?" I asked, I thought, with a folksy air.

"Few," he said. "Not many to know."

"Ever hear of a family named Cole?"

"Yup," he said. "That's most of 'em—"

"All the families in the county?"

"Just the important ones. Old Colonel Cole, he's the county judge."

"He's a lawyer?"

"Not so's you could tell," he shook his head and spat a mite of tobacco on the ground. "Don't have to be in these parts. He's military. A fly boy. Lots a medals and stuff. Born and raised right there in Bailey. Big old house outside town. Retired back there and ran for judge—give him something to do, I suppose."

"Got a wife?"

"Left her on one of his bases. Didn't see eye to eye, I guess."

"Family?"

"Got a daughter's all." He shook his head again, preparatory to the big spit that never came.

"Know anything about the daughter?"

"A handful I guess," he said, shaking his head. "Thought the old colonel could handle anything. Maybe met his match." When he completed his task I noticed he had taken pride in his work. In that moment I thought of him as a petroleum transfer engineer.

"Don't know what business you got with Colonel Cole, just a friendly piece of advice: Be careful. Got all votes but three. Talk is he know just who them three is, and I wouldn't envy being in their shoes. Better stay on the right side of the law, you ask me."

"Only three votes against?" I said. "Out of how many?"

"Five hundred or so—"

"That's all?"

"Only a thousand or so in the whole county. Bailey's the County Seat, gots 'bout half of 'em. Not the best half neither."

"What do people do for a living over there in Lucy County?"

"Got a speed trap, keeps things humming I expect."

"Oh? How's that?"

"You take them lines in the road. Most places you got a solid line, means don't pass. Broken line, passing okay. Now in Lucy, they reverse that. And they only paint the lines in places liable to mess up the drivers. Like on a long stretch of flat—they puts the broken lines. Then they got these old jalopies driving on them roads bout fifteen to twenty miles an hour. Folks passing left and right all day long. Peace officers hiding behind a billboard or something. Keeps the county treasury full up."

"So, all the thousand work on that scam?"

"Well, you got kids in there and welfare and Social Security. I imagine a few hundred's about it. Between keeping them lines painted, the jails workin', the justice of the peace—need four, round the clock—the traffic officers, the judge that's Colonel Cole, why, you got a pret-nice setup."

The old timer looked at me like I was crazy when I gave him an extra five dollars. He didn't seem to know what to do with it.

Passed over for the *Good Housekeeping* prize for tidiness, Sam Bast's Auto Repair Shop on the main drag (make that the only drag) in Bailey stood apart from the other necessaries of small-town living. There was a grocery, a dry goods store, a saloon and a church, and who could ask for anything more?

I felt like I was riding into town on a horse in one of those B-western movies. A couple of venerable citizens were killing their days on benches in front of the saloon, the grocery and the dry goods. There was no bench in front of the church. All loitering there was to be done inside.

Sam Bast's Auto Repair had no bench either, so the comely young woman was sitting on the hood of her car when I pulled up and parked in the street, so as to not interfere with any ingress or egress, as they say down at the courthouse.

I recognized her instantly from the photograph. Even though her clean khaki shorts and white tank top left her in a rather more modest condition than her boat ride photo, I realized mathematically the impossibility of there being two women who looked like that in a town like this.

When I strode into the repair garage as though I knew what I was doing, the beauty gave me what I thought was the come-hither eye—and I could do no less.

You've heard of bedroom eyes—Prudence had a bedroom smile. Come-hither lips that promised paradise. And boredom eyes.

I was drawn to her like a magnetic needle to the North Pole.

Alas, my progress in her direction was impeded by two figures of the male persuasion. It didn't take a rocket scientist to make them, as they say in the parlance of law enforcement. The guy in the greasy coveralls had to be Sam Bast, owner and chief executive officer of this fair establishment—short and jumpy, with a cigarette dangling from his moist lips.

The tall one was Judge Cole, father of Miss Tennessee on the car hood. He looked more military than judicial, and was not given to promiscuous smiling. His hair was uniformly jet black—which at his age could only have meant an intimacy with a shoe-polish bottle.

As soon as this statuesque heart-stopper cross-legged on the hood of the car felt her father's presence, her attitude toward me went south, all the way to Antarctica.

The judge looked at me like I was an intruder on a personal family affair. I suppose you might elevate car repairs to that strata, but I was not to be dissuaded.

"Prudence Cole, I presume," I said, with all the historical impact these words carried.

Her sidelong glance told me just what a pestiferous insect I was.

"Who wants to know?" Daddy Cole plowed in, apparently intending to intimidate.

Brightly, I stuck out my hand and shook his. "Gil Yates," I said, then added modestly, "private investigation."

We don't need any investigation around here," he said meaning to menace me with his tone.

"Yah never know," I chimed in with optimistic good cheer, and a touch of down-home accent.

It wasn't contagious.

The colonel fixed me in his bombsight and let go. "You're the guy who called yesterday—something about insurance."

"Insurance—not me." I looked at lovely on the hood of the car. "Did Les Quincy have insurance?"

"Not that I know of," Miss Tennessee said, as though I had said something insulting.

I didn't have to glance at the colonel to know he didn't believe me. He was glowering, but since we weren't in his courtroom, I felt reasonably secure.

"I wondered if I could ask you a few questions, Miss Cole?" I said.

Daddy answered for her. "You may not!"

"Oh, Daddy," she said. "He's so cute…"

"I'm well acquainted with your cute quotient, Prudence, and it's been nothing but trouble."

She flapped her eyelashes at me as though we were co-conspirators.

"What are the damages here, Sam?" The colonel/judge asked the proprietor, deciding to treat me like a fly in the ointment.

"Got the bill back in the office," he said. "Three hundred and something."

"Three hundred! Why the car's not worth that!"

"Is now," Sam said smiling sheepishly, his lips curling up around his ashy cigarette.

"I only came here to have the car fixed, I didn't want to buy your shop."

I looked around quickly and thought he would be overpaying for this place.

When I was fishing for something clever to say to wean Miss Beautiful from her daddy, a police car pulled into the driveway of Sam Bast's shop. It was closely followed by a long black Mercedes 600SL with smoked windows. It might have been the car responsible for Hitler's megalomania.

A uniformed officer got out of the police car, another out of the Mercedes. I later learned my surmise was correct. These two cops represented one hundred percent of the county law enforcement force.

The back door of the cop car was opened by the officer who drove it. He reached in and seemed to pull from within a swarthy character who might have traced his origins to the underside of the Middle East.

One look at him as he was dragged out like a sack of rutabagas and a blind man could have told he was not a happy camper.

"Here he is, Judge," the cop said, manhandling the outlaw, pushing him in front of Colonel Cole.

"This here's the judge," the cop said. "Start singing."

"Get these goddamn cuffs offa me. It's cruel and unusual punishment."

"I see you know our constitution," the judge

said, putting, I thought, a rather cruel and unusual inflection on the word *our*. "That may not do you much good around these parts. What's the beef?" he asked the officer.

"Speeding, passing in a no-passing zone. Resisting arrest. Tried to bribe me to let him go."

"Goddamn lies," the prisoner yelled so loud Judge Cole pulled his head back. "Watch your mouth," he said. "There's a lady present." The prisoner simmered for a moment, writhing his hands in the cuffs behind his back, as though he might wiggle free.

"Take the cuffs off," Colonel Cole said. "He's not going anywhere."

When the cuffs were off the prisoner flexed his fingers in front of him.

"Now young feller, what've you got to say for yourself?"

Well, he didn't say much, but he said it loud, peppered with a torrent of profanity as though showing the judge just what he thought of the "woman present" amid denials and accusations of being set up and trapped. His profane vocabulary was second to none, and I began to notice that every time he uttered another one Judge Cole lifted another finger until all ten had popped up twice.

"That's enough," he finally barked at the swarthy guy who suddenly seemed to give way his arrogance to fright. "I don't know where you come from, but around here we respect our women folk. No gentleman would talk that way in front of *any* lady. Now I'm going to give you a choice. Cool your heels and your mouth in the slammer awaiting some distant trial or pay your fine and get out of my county with your solemn promise never to darken our boundaries again."

The driver of the captured Mercedes nodded with a mixture of resignation and disgust. "How much is it?" he said reaching into his pocket. Both cops put their hands on their guns.

The judge looked him square in the eye, staring him down. "Five thousand dollars..."

"That's f...ing ridiculous," the prisoner yelled so loud the old timer in the gas station in the next county must have heard him.

"Shut up, you," Cole said firmly. Secure in his untouchable position. "That's the fine for the speeding, lane change and bribery. It's another twenty thousand to clean up your language. That's a thou a word just so's you'll know not to talk like that in front of ladies in my county."

"That's...ridiculous. I'm not paying anything like that—"

"Suit yourself. We have a pretty fair jail around here. You might get to like it—"

"Jail—?"

"Give us time to give your hearse here a good going over. See how a two-bit cracker like you can afford a Nazi car like Hitler."

The guy just glared at the judge. "I'll send you a check," he smirked.

Judge Cole shook his head without taking his eyes off his prey. "Cash," he said.

"Cash? You expect me to be driving around with that kind of cash?"

Cole looked levelly and showed him a smirk of his own. Then he nodded slowly. "Yeah, I expect you are."

The man blinked, giving the game away.

"But, hey, suit yourself. We can always impound your S.S. buggy here in lieu of cash."

There was a brittle standoff for a moment, but the driver knew he was trapped. He made one last run at it. "Got a bank here can cash a personal check that big?"

Colonel Cole sighed and shook his head. "Don't get it, do you?"

The decision made for him, the prisoner asked for his keys so he could open the trunk.

"We'll do it for you—"

Suddenly he became nervous as the cop with the keys went to his trunk. "Wait!" he said.

"Change your mind?"

"There's...personal stuff in there..."

Colonel Cole smiled, the knowing smile of the ages. "You think we're children here? You pay your fine, we aren't interested in personal belongings." Again the judge put the emphasis just askew enough to let us know he knew what was in the trunk.

The cop opened the trunk and stepped back, giving the Middle Easterner access. A cliché black attache case appeared from under a blanket. He opened it and took out three neatly tied bundles of bills.

He sat them aside, locked the case, then the trunk. He turned and handed the two packs to Judge Cole, then broke the band around the third pack and counted out five thousand—and handed it to the judge with a smirk.

"You going to give me a receipt?" he asked.

"No receipt," the judge says.

"How do I know you won't stop me again?"

"You don't know—but it's lunchtime—that's

enough time for you to get out of my county. 'Sides," he said with a smile, "my word is my bond…"

The arestee got into the car like a John rabbit and drove off, but not at any obscene rate of speed.

I watched Prudence during this playlet and saw she was pleased to be the center of this flurry of activity.

The judge counted out four one hundred dollar bills and handed them to Sam Bast, proprietor. "There you go, Sam—a little extra for your trouble."

Sam was astonished. Prudence asked her father, "What you going to do with the rest of that, Daddy?"

"Give it to the American Legion, I expect. He wanted a receipt," he said, laughing. He was so proud of himself, he seemed to forget Prudence and me.

"Come on into the office," Sam chuckled, "I'll give you your receipt." The two men disappeared into the hovel off the repair pits.

Prudence slid off the hood and moved gracefully over to where I stood on the sidelines.

"Let's go for a walk," she said.

We repaired to a stream behind the auto shop. It was green and humid and buggy. I always wondered what the flies did when I wasn't around. They seemed to favor me, circling, buzzing incessantly as though I were the prize meat.

"So, you're here about Les Quincy," she said. She was not a delicate southern flower like her daddy seemed to think, but a young woman who seemed to have a good grasp on life. My first impression by the stream was that she had taken some knocks in her time, and she had learned how to take care of herself.

And she was a looker. On her feet, she was fairly tall with a ruddy round face and a well-proportioned frame—though that goes without saying for a Les Quincy crew member.

"Well, how do you like our little town?" she asked, as we wended our way down the tangled bank to the stream.

"I've never seen anything like it," I said. "I come from urban sprawl, wall-to-wall housing. This is sort of nice, I guess."

"If you don't care about modern conveniences like going to the movies."

"What did you make of that scene with the Mercedes guy?"

"Oh, that was just Daddy showing off his power. But he's an old-fashioned southern gentleman where ladies are concerned."

"But isn't he afraid of reprisals?"

"My daddy fears no man. He's military to the core. Why, every night he goes out back and shoots off his gun just to warn anybody who's got any ideas—Daddy means business."

"How does he compare to Captain Les Quincy?"

She gave a short projectile laugh. "No comparison," she said. "Les had to surround himself with compliant, unthreatening women to make him macho. Daddy *is* macho."

"Any ideas how Les died?"

"Nothing worth anything," she said. "I speculated some, but there's nothing to back it up."

The water moseyed along the rocks in the stream in no hurry to get anywhere.

"What did you speculate?" I asked.

"I think we were knocked out for starters."

"Drugged?"

She nodded. "We all slept like logs—that is—far as I know. Apparently, one of us *didn't* sleep."

"Who do you think that was?"

"I don't know."

"Theories?"

"Of course."

"Who?"

She held up a hand to stop my prying. "Maybe later," she said. "Come on over here, I want to show you a special place I come to meditate." We made our way along the edge of the stream, and I could see getting used to this kind of life—but not if I were a young woman. A sea adventure was certainly understandable.

We came to a sheltered clearing away from the sparse building of "downtown" Bailey, and Prudence sank to the ground in a semiswoon. She patted the earth next to her. "Here," she said. "Sit here."

I sat next to her. She had a smile of contentment on her face. "You have pretty blue eyes," she said. "I don't think I've ever *seen* such pretty blue eyes."

She leaned back on her elbows while staring at me and pointing up some of her finer points which were halfheartedly covered with a sheer white blouse.

"Do you remember anything about your last night on board?"

"Not much. I was out like a light."

"Remember who did the cooking that last night?"

"Sure. It was Kay."

"Kay? She told me she didn't remember. Thought it might have been Ruth."

"Oh," she said, raising an eyebrow. "You talked to Kay already?" She seemed disappointed Kay had upstaged her.

I felt called upon to explain. "I was in Honolulu," I shrugged. "She was closest."

"That's all right," Prudence said. "I'm not *too* jealous." She looked away from me. "It was Kay who cooked that night."

"You're sure?"

"Of course, I'm sure. She did so damn little that I couldn't forget her doing anything. I think she traded with someone."

"So, what was it like? What did you eat?"

"Some kind of pasta. Hard to tell what it was. Kay wasn't much of a cook."

"What else do you remember?"

"I could hardly get myself into bed fast enough. The other girls too. I'm not sure about Kay," she wrinkled her brow in thought.

"How about Quincy?"

"Him too."

"You tell the police this?"

"Pretty much." She looked at me with come-hither eyes. "I'd tell *you* more," she said. "You have *such* pretty eyes."

"So, you don't know if Kay was as sleepy as the rest of you?"

"No."

"She said you all were always tired. Hard days—hot sun—motion of the boat. That true?"

"Oh, sure—but this was different. I'd swear we were given something."

"When did you wake up?"

"Next morning. It was light. Don't remember what time. I didn't pay much attention to time on the boat. I was running away from time. It was my whole purpose being there—to forget that lump of a husband I'd just chucked. Daddy told me not to marry him and he was right. I didn't even wear my watch the whole time I was on the boat."

"If you had to guess—what time did you get up that last day?"

"Six-thirty to seven-thirty."

"What time was dinner?"

"Around eight."

"And Ruth cooked?" I said trying to be scatter-brained.

"No, Kay."

"She told me Ruth."

"She probably told you Les was marrying her, too."

"Well, now that you mention it…"

Prudence shook her head with vigor. "No way," she said. "For starters, he was already married."

"Kay said he was getting a divorce."

Prudence smirked. "Maybe so—but not to marry *her.*"

"Someone else?"

"Maybe…"

"You?"

"You kidding? He was rude, crude and unattractive. Just Kay's type—*not* mine."

"Another crew member?"

"Oh," she waved a dismissive hand, "he had that way about him—you know—every girl is the only girl. There we are—five of us, and we rotate like his own private whorehouse, only we don't get paid. Laid but not paid," she rolled her eyes. "So he's got to have a good time. I mean, those were pretty close quarters and we had to work together—it was matter of life and death—and you get competing women in that situation and it's got to be explosive—we had five."

"So, it was dynamite?"

"There was tension in the beginning. Like we each wanted to be his favorite."

"You too?" I asked.

She flipped a shoulder. "Sure, me too. You get a man and two or more women, you have built-in competition—that's in *normal* circumstances. Here we were cooped up in a thirty-five foot boat. I mean, that was our world. So, yeah, we were all out for the prize."

"Even Ruth?"

"The Jesus freak? My God, I'd be hard pressed...but, yeah, I'd say, even Ruth in her way."

"What was her way?"

"God and Jesus. Maybe her goal wasn't to have him love her best and exclusively—and walk down the aisle with him in a pure-white gown. Maybe she didn't care about winning his heart for her personally—but for God and Jesus."

I was amazed at how eager women were to cat about other women they saw as competitors, given the least opportunity. "What about the other girls?"

"They were in there swinging. Like I say, we were wary in the beginning, then after only a couple days or so we had, or thought we had, a pretty good fix on the others."

"So, for all intensive purposes, you were one happy family?"

Prudence exploded with laughter.

"What's so funny?"

"Oh nothing. It's just—"

"What?"

"What you said. All intensive purposes. That cliché goes *intents* and purposes. But you know, it may be better in this case your way. Anyway—what were they like? A real mixed bag, which convinced me he only picked us for our bodies. We had nothing else in common. There was Ruth who read the Bible all day and got down on her goddamn knees at night to pray," she shuddered at the memory.

"Then there was Elizabeth-Don't-Call-Me-Betty-It-Rhymes-With-Petty. She was a criminal from all I could tell of the tales she told. She was running from the cops. Some drug thing she blamed on a boyfriend or something. Played real innocent. Like she was Miss Gullible. I didn't buy it—I guess we were all running from something."

"You?"

"Sure."

"What?"

"A destroyed marriage. Waiting here in God's forgotten land for a miracle I didn't find."

"And Sooshe."

"Oh, God, Sooshe. Same. An abusive boyfriend. God, could she talk. Les got her pregnant you know."

"Kay said—"

"Wanted her to abort. She wouldn't hear of it. Like she thought she'd never get another chance. Now or never."

"You'd have aborted?"

"I wouldn't get in that fix—not with that creep."

"So, who'd want to kill him?"

"All of us," she answered without hesitation. "No question."

"What do you think happened?"

She shrugged. "He disappeared. There at night, gone in the morning."

"Any speculation?"

"Sure, I've done some. One idea is someone

came for him. His debtors were closing in, his wife was on the rampage, why not run off, get a new identity?"

"Just abandon the boat? Was he independently wealthy?"

"I don't know. Or one of us could have killed him and thrown him over the side. Maybe he'll wash up sometime, if the sharks haven't gotten him."

"Who?"

"That's a big question," she said. "Who? Well, not me. I didn't care about him enough to kill him."

"Ruth?"

"Geez, probably no one less likely. God wouldn't approve—'Thou shalt not kill,' and all that. But," she shrugged, "stranger things have happened. 'Hell hath no fury like a woman scorned' my daddy always says. Lot of 'em in *that* boat."

"Meaning?"

"Well, Kay, I don't care what she says—she *was* scorned. She made the biggest play for him. It was so obvious it was embarrassing. She had the dream he was going to marry her, but I knew that's all it was, a dream. Once scorned.

"Sooshe wanted a daddy to go with her child. He wanted it aborted. Two scorned.

"He relieved Ruth of her virginity. She wanted a commitment in return. He might have promised it to her to take her prize. Wouldn't put it past him."

"Elizabeth?"

"Oh, I don't know. She was such a hard-bitten bitch—but," she added as though she just thought of it, "she is a woman after all, and maybe she felt scorned by the musical beds."

"Did you?"

"Oh, I suppose at first. Then I thought, what the hell, relax and enjoy it."

"Did you?"

"Not often, really," she said. "He was such a creep."

"Kay said she developed exclusive rights at the end. Is that right?"

"Kay had delusions—she was a pain where you can't see it from here." Prudence put her hand with a loving caress on the soft tissue behind her. Then her leg strayed in my direction. She kicked off her shoe and began rubbing her foot up and down my leg.

I think I must have made some inappropriate sounds because I heard a rustling of the underbrush, and I looked up to see one of those nice policemen coming toward me as though he'd just spotted public enemy number one.

He grabbed my arm, just as it had frozen in the encircling of Prudence's waist. He pulled me up so hard I was sure my arm had separated from its socket.

"Hey!" I groaned.

"Come on, you," he said, as thought I were some anonymous miscreant. "Got a message for you."

I glanced back at Prudence as I was being rather unceremoniously led up the primrose path.

She was smiling, as though she had put another one over on the authorities.

He didn't speak to me until we got back to my car, where he opened the door and threw me, unsociable like, onto the driver's seat.

He leaned over me, and said with redneck menace, "Got a message for you from the judge. It goes like this: 'You go messing with my little girl, I'll hound you to the ends of the earth. Won't be no place you can hide from my wrath.'"

The tin horn looked me in the eye. "Get it?" he asked.

I got it.

11

I didn't dawdle. She was a looker, but my survival still held a fascination for me. I may have flown higher in that car back to Nashville than I did in the plane to New Orleans, from then another rental, obtained, as usual, by perfervid comparative shopping. On to Baton Rouge, the evangelism capital of the world.

There was something about the bayou—all that swamp land—that didn't feel hospitable. Youthful movies about folks disappearing in quicksand might have had something to do with it. But if the truth were known, the smell wasn't pleasant, and I wondered if that had anything to do with the popularity of fundamental religion in this neck of the world.

The last known address for Ruth Waters was an apartment not too close to the heart of things.

It was obvious God watered the grass here and She had fallen down on the job lately.

The painter also seemed to have been on hiatus. In *sum*: not what you would call upscale.

My persistent knocking was answered, not from

within, but from a husky, androgynous voice behind me on the sorry lawn. It belonged to the manager—a down-at-the-mouth woman who sought to seriously grasp the world before it strangled her.

"No one there," she said, coming at me obliquely and startling me with the heavy sound of her voice.

"Ruth Waters?" I said hopefully.

"Gone," she said.

"Know where?"

She shook her head. "Up an' gone. Went on some kinda boat trip out by Hawaii an' she never came back."

"What happened to her stuff?"

"Boyfriend took it."

"Boyfriend?" I asked. "Longterm thing?"

"All the time they was here," she said. "Going on two years, I expect."

"Get along, did they?"

"Far's I know. They was religious types. Students out at the Bible College."

"Good Christian folk," I said, more as a musing than as a question. "Know where the boyfriend moved to?"

"Lemme see if I gots his address," she turned and lumbered back to the door with the plastic cut-out sign that said "Office."

I don't know why the words 'Darkness shall cover the earth,' came to mind on being invited into the manager's apartment. Well, yes I do. It was dark; a repository of knickknacks and piles of paper. She took a load off her feet and sat at a desk a lot smaller than it needed to be and rummaged through papers until she hit payroll dirt.

"Here it is," she said, stirring the papers on the desk until she found paper and pen. Putting paper under pen, she wrote his name and address. "Don't know if he has a phone." She gave me directions to Mark's place.

I thanked her and climbed back in the car.

Over dale and down a few hills I came to a rural section with small houses and relatively large lots, but no evidence of farming—unless you counted junk cars in the front on blocks, old refrigerators and stoves taking the sun.

I pulled up to the address in hand, got out of the car and made my way over some dead grass to the front door. I knocked and soon discovered there didn't seem to be anyone home but the flies.

On a hunch, I tread lightly around to the back of the house where I was startled to see a comely nude sunbathing, bottoms up, on a blanket.

Now what? I couldn't see scaring her, she must have been asleep. I couldn't see embarrassing her, and I thought it presumptuous to cover her up, especially since there didn't seem to be anything to cover her with.

I cleared my throat and turned my back to her.

Nothing.

"Ruth?" I said to the neighbor's backyard.

I heard a rustling, then the sound of gasping surprise. "Don't you knock?" she reprimanded me.

"I did," I said weakly, without turning to face her.

"It's okay," she said. "You can turn around."

I did so, very slowly. She was sitting up, her

arms circling her tented legs so the real private stuff was kept private. "Ruth?" I said, but before she corrected me I saw she didn't look like my pictures of Ruth.

"I'm Lisa," she said. "No Ruth here."

"Hi," I said with an all-outdoors smile. "I'm Gil. You don't know Ruth Waters?"

She shook her head.

"Mark?" I said. "Know if Mark lives here?"

"Yeah, what you want with him?"

"It's Ruth I'm looking for. I thought Mark might know where to find her."

She shrugged. "Couldn't prove it by me."

"You living with Mark?"

"Off and on," she said. "I go to school mostly."

"Oh, where?"

"Over by the Baton Rouge Bible College."

All the cracks that came to mind about Adam and Eve I suppressed. I didn't even ask if her teachers sanctioned nudity. It was hard to keep up with modern religion.

"Know where I can find Mark?"

"Ought to be home anytime now. Want to come in and wait? I could give you something cold..." she tilted her head to look at me through some pretty robust eyelashes..."or *hot* if you prefer." The inflection she put on 'hot' left me quivering.

"Sounds...nice," I said. I watched her get to her feet making a careless attempt to cover her biblical nakedness with the blanket. That she was inept at it didn't bother me at all.

She was short on her feet, but the religious tanning had taken hold. Her figure was not too shabby.

"Excuse me while I put something on," she said

and took two steps to the couch where a long tee shirt reposed. On the front it said, Jesus Loves me. She picked it up and put it over her head while the blanket slid uninhibitedly to the floor. I tried to fake looking the other way but the effort met with only partial success. On the wall was an eight-by-ten picture of Jesus—white, male and forlorn in the huge space. A titled Madonna and child adorned another wall. The third wall had some dude I didn't recognize—possibly a big artificial hair at the bible college. The fourth wall had the window looking out on the dead grass.

"Now," she said. "What do...you...want?"

"I..."

"To drink."

"Oh, just water," I said. Can you be relieved and disappointed at the same time? She was gallivanting around the tiny house in this tee shirt that left nothing to the imagination upstairs and barely covered downstairs.

She produced a Mason jar of water and tittered, "You like our fine china?"

"I like it fine," I said.

"You look tired," she said. "Long trip?"

"Oh," I flushed. "No, I'm not...ah, tired. The trip wasn't bad—except I don't care for flying."

"Yeah? Me neither," she said lighting up as though we had enough in common to get married. "I just thought you might like to rest till Mark gets back."

"Oh, no thanks, I'm fine."

Lisa pouted, as though I'd insulted her.

I don't know how we got through the next half hour until the man himself came home. Lisa did her best to keep my mind off Ruth, and every other woman

I'd ever known the way she slithered around in the chair facing me, giving me peeks at all her secrets. By the time Mark walked in my breath was about gone and my heartbeat was miles down the street.

Mark was a medium tall, skinny guy with Dumbo ears. He seemed startled to see me with Lisa in those vestments, and I couldn't blame him.

I jumped up, perhaps a tad heavy on the conviviality, stuck out my hand and said with a nervous irrationality, "Mark? I'm Gil Yates, I just came to town looking for Ruth Waters, but she's apparently moved. Her landlady was kind enough to give me your address. I hope you don't mind I came right out, and Lisa here has been most gracious in allowing me to wait for you."

He cast a glance at Lisa, then looked back at me with a glance that did not bespeak trust.

"Ruth's gone," he said in a flat down-home voice, like he was telling me they were temporarily out of milk.

"Know where?"

He shook his head, and I didn't see anything there to make me doubt him.

"You have time to answer a few questions about her?" I asked, humble chiffon pie all over my face.

"Lord willing, I got lots a time," he said, then he gave me the fish eye. "What you want with Ruth?"

"Just talk to her," I said.

"What about?" You could have cut the suspicion in his voice with a buzz saw.

"She went on a boat trip awhile back. The captain disappeared. The police report didn't satisfy his wife." I tossed the whole idea off like yesterday's laundry. "Hired me to find out what I could."

He jerked his head once. "Can't help none. I don't know nothin' 'bout no disappearance." Without facing Lisa, he said, "Honey, how about a Coke for me and Mr. Gil—"

Honey jumped up and took the few steps to the refrigerator.

"Oh, water's fine," I said.

"I'll have Coke," Mark said, then seemed to settle into the couch like icing covering a cake. "Ruth..." he said and sighed, trying to recreate a cleansed memory. "Ruth," he said again. "I expect Ruth has gone to hell."

"Oh? Why?"

"I tried to stop her from going with that Satan in Hawaii. Can you just imagine what kinda business that was? Five girls and a stud." He shook his head. "Can you just imagine," he said again, showing a certain lack of imagination of his own, "what the good Lord must think of that operation?"

Lisa returned to plop a can of Coke in Mark's hand. He took it without comment; he seemed perturbed she hadn't opened it. He did so and took a long swallow.

"How long did you know Ruth?" I said.

"Oh, three, four years. We were going to be married—till she got that fool idea in her head."

"How did she hear about it?"

"Got a sister out in California saw an ad in a paper. Joked about it to Ruth, but Ruth took it serious. I'm blessed if she didn't send a dirty picture of herself looking like a Jezebel and didn't he just rise to the bait. Somehow she made the cut and off she went to Sodom and Gomorrah. I told her in no uncertain terms it was the work of Satan, and his hand would be guiding that sinful boat through hell's waters."

"A-men," said the resident Jezebel.

"Do you know anything about her sister? Where she lives, her name?"

"Someplace in California. San something. Was married once: don't know her last name."

Big help, I thought.

"Did you hear from her after she left?" I asked.

"Oh, yes, I did. Got a whole stack of letters from her saying I was right all along, and this captain, he was a demon—the way he abused the womenfolk. Talking all the time like she wanted to get off, but there was just no way on God's green earth that she could bring off an escape. Sometimes, she confessed, she prayed to God in Heaven to take the skipper's life—but He didn't want him—until the end, of course."

"Did she come back here?" I asked, trying to hide my excitement about the letters.

"She did not. She knew she was not welcome. She was a sinner."

"Doesn't God forgive sinners?" I asked, with just an innocent touch of naïveté.

"I expect God forgives, yes sir. I just didn't find it in my heart."

"Besides," Lisa said. "You met me."

"Hush, you," he hissed. "Go get yourself decent."

"I am decent," she said, casting a seductive eye in my direction. "You don't mind, do you?"

She'd put me on the spot. Of course, I agreed with her. Not only didn't she bother me, I found her quite an attraction. On the other hand, I wanted to get my hands on those letters and I had the strong feeling I'd have a better chance if I agreed with him.

The best I could do was a noncommittal shrug. "Tell me about the letters," I said.

"Not much," he twisted his nose showing a limber faculty in that regard. "Gabbing on about the big Satan and his prey. Trying to win me back."

"How so?" I asked.

"When she had her mind set on this fool voyage, I told her in no uncertain terms, the Lord would no more sanction these goings on than he did the debauchery at Sodom and Gomorrah—and neither would I. If she had her mind set on such foolishness, she needn't come back."

So much for Christian compassion, I thought. Taking the cow by the ears, I said, "Can I see those letters?" deliberately compromising my grammar to disarm him.

He turned up his nose. "What you want with them letters?"

I wondered if he realized he was making the idea more enticing. "Might give me a clue about what happened."

He thought a minute. Looked over at Jezebel-in-residence as though she might be hiding the answer. "Well," he said at last, "I don't think so. Them letters is private. I don't want to go getting Ruth in any more trouble than she's already in."

Lisa signaled me—pointing to her chest with her thumb and mouthing the words "I'll get them for you." Then she pointed at me as if I might have missed the idea.

I looked around the room as if to say, How are

you going to do it?

Mark, self-possessed, was droning on about what a Satan Les Quincy was and what a Jezebel Ruth was, and I listened politely if not intently. After the third Coke did its work and Mark ducked into the bathroom, Lisa leaped up and went into what I took to be the bedroom. I heard a drawer scraping just when I heard the toilet flushing. She darted back to the living room and stuffed a manila envelope down the front of my pants. She sat back down just as the door to the bathroom opened and Mark came out pulling up his fly zipper.

He pounced back down on the chair as though he had a grudge against it, while I was trying to figure out how I could get out of there without letters dropping from my pants legs.

I finally settled on an idea: I put my hands in my pockets and got a grip on the envelope from both sides. Before too long, I garnered the nerve to stand up.

"Well, thanks for the help," I said.

"Didn't give you much," Mark said.

If he only knew.

I headed for the Baton Rouge Bible College, which used to be named for a high profile evangelist before his Byzantine libido unfurled itself in public. The survivors thought it best to disassociate the institution from the carnal cleric with a less disastrous generic name.

The campus had a nice sprawl to it. They obviously didn't buy land by the square foot here.

Naturally the young, pimply-faced woman in the registrar's office said, "We don't give out that information."

So, I gave her a corny smile and did the insurance dance: "She's the beneficiary of a large insurance policy," I said, rather cleverly, "and I can't locate her. All my leads led me here."

"Sorry."

"Tell you what," I said. "I'm not at liberty to discuss the amount in question, other than to say it is quite substantial. Because of the difficulty in locating this particular beneficiary, I am authorized to pay a reward equivalent to one year's pay of the person who sets me on the right path."

I watched her jaw working. I could imagine the saliva glands pumping away. It wasn't my choice to pull this on such an innocent—but who else would go for it?

She turned out to be not quite as dumb as I thought she was. She left the counter quietly, went in the back and rifled though a few records and returned with some information written on a piece of paper. I tried to see what it said, but she was playing it close to the chest.

"May I have your card?" she said.

Naturally—thou shalt not live by faith alone, someone in her line of work might have said sometime.

"You know," I said earnestly, "I'm in such a confidential line of work, they don't permit me to have cards. However, I'll trade you your info for mine. Even up. Fair enough?"

She was skeptical. Who wouldn't be? Her questioning gaze into my eyes seemed eternal. She was my daughter's age, and I was unnerved. Not much of a liar was I.

Merely to divert my mind, I took out a scrap of paper and wrote:

Horace Ableman
Insurance Investigator

to which I added a bogus telephone number.

She tried to see it. I pressed it to my chest. "Uh, uh," I said. "Trade?"

Our eyes locked for another moment. Then with a shrug, she pushed her paper at me across the counter.

I did likewise. I read mine, smiled and turned on my heels before she could get to a phone.

Back in the car, I headed for the airport in New Orleans for the flight home. The addresses I had on the three remaining shapely sailors were all within driving distance of my hometown, and I needed the time to get past my oblivious wife and insufferable father-in-law/boss.

I waited until I was on the plane to read Ruth's letters. I hoped it would take my mind off the terrors of flying.

Behind me sat a young boy—too young to fly unattended, for he kept kicking the back of my seat with intermittent abandon. But what could you expect in an oxygen-deprived environment?

Next to me was a young man on the go with not the slightest sense of privacy. He spent much of the trip telephoning around the country, speaking of his deals and his sexual conquests.

The Letters of Ruth were a balm to my sanity:

Ruth's letters were chatty, therapeutic pieces sprinkled with religious sentiment, some piety and thinly veiled pitches for reconciliation, return mail and simple reassurance, which was apparently not forthcoming from the stern recipient, Mark.

Dearest Mark (Matthew, Luke and John, too?),

I know how you feel about me taking this trip and how you gave me an ultimatum and all, but I just can't get you out of my mind. It's so lonely here—even though there are six of us on a thirty-five foot boat, these people are not like any I have ever known, so for my own peace of mind I am writing these letters—like sort of a diary—and I will send them to you, even though I know you probably won't bother to read them since I disappointed you so!

My fellow crew members are a heathen lot. I know you told me it would be like this, but I guess I had to see for myself. It sure is a different crowd than the Baton Rouge Bible College. I pray to God every night that I survive the trip. My prayers and these letters to you are all that keep me going. And I know you've put me out of your heart, even though Jesus forgave the sinners and even though I stoutly proclaim Jesus Christ as my personal savior—now more than ever.

My eyes have been opened. I'm a new woman. I think of you always and chastise myself daily for leaving you for this adventure and these...strange people. I thought I needed some space and there's no more space than the ocean. But I've never been in a more suffocating environment.

The Captain, Les Quincy, I told you about. He is a big mouth, who demands absolute obedience.

He soon learned I wouldn't be treated like part of his personal harem and when it was my "turn" I slept on the floor. Fortunately for him the other four are willing, so outside of rude remarks and suggestive comments, he has left me pretty much alone. Oh, I still have my place in his "sleeping order," but I don't take it and he knows I won't.

The other four are a strange mix. All they have in common are nice bodies and pretty faces. One of them, Kay, is married and has two kids, who she's left with her estranged husband while she has a good time. Another, Prudence (who is anything but prudent) is divorced. Sooshe is like a hippie. She's a nude model in real life and is, according to her, pregnant by our captain, who is not happy about it.

Last, and maybe least, is Elizabeth, who I think is simply a criminal. Most of her friends seem to be in jail, and she may be on this trip to escape jail herself. Lots of drugs and stuff. So you can see why I need to pray.

There is something strange going on here. My fellow females hate me for being different. Seems my chastity makes them feel guilty. They are civil to me—except Elizabeth—but aloof. I don't know what is eating Elizabeth, I've never said boo to her. I think she's just uncomfortable around anyone who has God by her side. She could use Him, believe me, and I think she knows it. When ever I bring up God or Jesus, she'll make some sarcastic remark.

And before we got out of range, Les had

some pretty heavy screaming matches on his cell phone. He was in his cabin with the door closed so I couldn't hear what he was saying, but the tone was unmistakable—furious.

I don't know when I'll get to mail these letters. Les keeps us in the dark about when and where we'll be in port. I think somewhere in Japan is going to be our first stop, now that we've left the islands.

The captain bugs. He won't leave me alone. It's like he's made it his mission to defile me. He's not satisfied to have every other woman on the boat. I've become his particular challenge.

"Try it," he says. "You'll like it."

"Most beautiful thing in life," he says.

I tell him, "That's if it is someone you love—someone you are married to for the glory of God."

He makes fun of me. Calls me a mal-adjusted old maid.

I won't give in.

It is shameful to see these women carry on over this horrid man.

When I had the interview and I asked if there'd be any reason to be afraid, he laughed and said, "You'll outnumber me, five to one."

Well, he'd done it before. He knew that five women competing to be number one were no match for the one man who knew how to operate the boat. In whose hands we had naïvely placed our lives.

In our case it's four hens at each other over the cock of the walk. Oh, it's subtle, the digs, the backbiting, but it's unmistakable.

Last night it was my night with the captain. I was out on the deck as always and I hear quite a goings on, like they were all having a party. I crept over to the hatch and looked down—and I could see the merest hint of goings on in the captain's quarters. There they all were, naked as the day they were born, having this Godless orgy, and I know you would like it better if I didn't say so, but I had these strange stirrings—urges even, so I had to stop looking. I went back to my makeshift bedding and tried to shut my eyes and ears, but truth be known, none of us got much sleep last night.

This morning Captain Les told me I missed a fun party.

I said I do not do Satan's work and he laughed and said it wasn't work, it was play. Then he said I shouldn't be so uptight—I'd die an old maid without ever experiencing the fun in life.

I am more resolved than ever not to have anything more to do with him than I have to.

My concentration was broken by the guy sitting next to me. He was in big mouth city, as the young at heart might say. The phone was bobbing on his ear as he ducked and raised his head during his logorrhea.

I tried to signal Casanova with a withering frown, but time and bitter experience had built in him an imperious immunity.

Old Les didn't sound like every woman's dream, but he sure knew how to get women. It put me in mind of a book I read, title "Nice Guys Don't Get Laid." In the real world, I'm a nice guy.

Did Ruth have just cause to ship Lucky Les to dreamland? My seatmate took a breather while obviously searching for the someone else to call. I picked up the next letter and read on.

Things have gone sour on the ship since the orgy. The life of the devil is beginning to catch up with them all. The girls are at each other more than ever. Kay has weaseled more time with Les than Sooshe, Elizabeth and Prudence. Sooshe is fit to be tied since she is carrying Les's baby. Funny, she was all right with it while she was sharing him equally, but when he starts to show favoritism to someone else, she goes bananas. She said to me, "I could kill him!" Not that I think she would.

I miss you terribly. My life just isn't the same without you. This impulse to join this crew was a big mistake. And I must resign myself that I will never live it down as far as you are concerned.

Les is still at me, even though he has, for now, settled in with Kay. It's like I'm this big challenge for him.

But the more he comes on to me, the firmer my resolve to have nothing to do with him.

Dear God, keep me strong. Don't let me weaken and fall into the clutches of Satan.

Father forgive me. I have sinned. I couldn't help myself, I fell headlong into the arms of Satan and I am so ashamed.

But the strangest thing, the other girls are furious at Les for taking advantage of me. It seems they respected my position and think Les is a skunk for forcing himself on me. They all walked into the fire with their eyes open, Prudence said, but I am put upon, constantly belittled, given extra work, and the worst like cleaning the head and washing the dishes in the galley.

I have half a notion if we knew more about the ship's operation there might be a mutiny. I think Les keeps us in the dark on purpose.

Things are getting intolerable aboard the fun house. Les seems to be going mad. His demands are outrageous, illogical. He calls fire drills in the middle of the night and we all have to tumble out of bed, half naked, just for his pleasure. He makes us bend over in our short nightgowns on the flimsiest pretenses. Some of the girls laugh, but I don't think it's one bit funny.

It's begun to seem like our captain has lost his mind. He laughs like a hyena at the stupidest things. His actions are irrational, his movements jerky, his orders unreasonable and unpredictable.

Here the letters ended abruptly. There may have been more, but this was all I got.

Ruth had some explaining to do. I was eager to meet her.

In spite of the pilot's best efforts to kill me in some horrendous winds, with lightening flashing about, I arrived at the LAX airport to tell the tale.

I retrieved my car from Lot C and drove home. When I saw Tyranny's car in the driveway, I headed to the office—though it is a tossup which of the Wemples is least congenial. Daddy Pimple was a tad farther removed and so I was able to be slightly more objective. With time, I had concluded Daddybucks was really a figure of fun and I should be able to step back and laugh at him.

If only I didn't work for him.

"*Malvin!* Where the Sam Hill you been? We're in deep doodoo out on Artesia. Some idiot was planting a tree and cut the main line. Not pretty! Who the Sam Hill authorized you to go planting trees?"

"Made the executive decision," I shrugged.

After twenty-some years, I was finally taking it on myself to spend fifty dollars here and there without running to the micromanager here on his platform first. He didn't like it.

Tough.

"Trying to drive me to the poorhouse? You want to smother *your* house with palm trees, that's your affair. You seen one tree, you seen 'em all. So, get out there and put your finger on the dike, Boy."

Down at my desk, a few steps lower than the exalted high potentate, I called the manager. She had taken care of the pipe break and everything was back to normal. Daddy Wimp was so dramatic.

Behind me the cream of Elbert A. Wemple Ass. Realtors were chugging away. Like prize cows, they were the "top producers" who kept E. August sitting on his fat fanny twelve inches above the rest of us. If he ever had lungs like his daughter, Dorcas, they had slipped.

And, speaking of Dorcas, My Tyranny Rex, she was my next hurdle.

I've found that nothing is so conducive to clearing emotional baggage from one's thought than a mosey in my palm and cycad garden(s). Now plural because I bought the house next door with my handsome fee from the megabucks, Harold Mattlock.

It was amazing how effortlessly you could blow thousands on these little cycads—plants which reminded the unwashed of stunted palms.

I checked my new *Encephalartos latifrons* and *Encephalartos poggei,* my four-thousand dollar beauties. They looked much the same, but the leaves were turning brown. I'd have to cut them off, leaving me with a bare lump of a caudex until they took an inkling to bloom. Maybe this year, maybe not.

Either that babe at the Bible College tricked me more than I tricked her, or Ruth had vaporized. Ruth wasn't at the address she gave me and they had never heard of her. Which in retrospect was, I suppose, fair enough, since she wouldn't be coming into any chunk of dough from an insurance company.

Santa Barbara, next stop. Sooshe Jenkins. The hills above town where some years before the hippies took a foothold. The hippies, you may recall, rebelled at conformity, and they suffered badly those who did not rebel in the same manner.

The address I had was up one of those climbing, winding roads, narrow but asphalt for awhile, then just narrow dirt until you thought you were going to fall off the end of the earth.

The shack I found there in the chapparal was obviously out of reach of any building and safety department, and I couldn't blame them. I barely survived the adventure myself.

Unhappily, since a good sneeze would have blown the house down (no huffing and puffing necessary) there was no one inside.

Back in the car, I rode the brakes down to the nearest neighbor. The sound of a numbing bongo rhythm was in the air. It was amazing how this guy could keep pounding the same rhythm endlessly—and what a generous spirit he was to do it outside where everyone for miles could hear it. The hills acted as an amphitheater, amplifying every sound.

I wasn't sanguine about getting any useful information from the bongo banger. From the look of him hunched over his drums in the backyard, he didn't have much truck with anyone unless you happened to be a bongo drum.

Fortunately his long suffering mother was...long

suffering. She wore a well-worn granny dress and had frayed, stringy hair, and told me in a weary tone that her neighbor, Sooshe, was modeling for adult education sculpture classes. She even gave me directions—back down the hill and into town.

I pulled into the parking lot of the Schott Center and found my way to Room 4. The doors were closed. All the other classroom doors were open.

While I stood there wondering if I should knock, the door opened as an older gentleman came out. I held it and walked in. There was a young woman I recognized as Sooshe sitting in the center of the room on a platform, her chin on her palm, her elbow on her knee—naked as a wren-tit.

Circled around her was a class of twenty men and women intent on molding lumps of clay on the stands in front of them into looking more or less like Sooshe.

I looked at Sooshe for signs of self-conscious discomfort but found none. The clock on the wall said a few minutes before twelve and she was chatting away with some of the student artists—who seemed to be made up largely of what we euphemistically refer to as seniors.

Sooshe was thin with prominent breasts, a narrow, sloping face and dirty-blond hair tied in a ponytail in back. Her legs, arms and torso were so thin I questioned her nutrition. I expect it was deliberate, fat being the scourge of the modeling profession.

On the stroke of noon, she stood up, grabbed a sack dress and threw it over her head.

A male dropout from the hippie culture appeared with a baby and handed it to Sooshe. Mr.

Hippie was disheveled and dispirited with dirty blond hair and dirty bare feet, I could tell he felt babysitting was just a notch below his dignity. But she was bringing home the bacon, lettuce and tomato, so what could he do?

Sooshe sat back down on the platform, unbuttoned the top of the dress, and uncovered her breast with some modesty in spite of the display we'd all had of both of them a minute ago, and began nursing this kid.

The class was packing up to leave when I sauntered over to Sooshe to introduce myself.

She smiled. "Oh, God," she said, "that trip. I've been trying to forget it." Sooshe was friendly and casual—loose of joints and spirit.

I looked at the suckling babe. "I'm told Les Quincy is his father."

She paused. "He's Les's all right," she said, rolling her eyes at the memory. "At first he didn't want to admit it—denied it. Said I was 'active.' Well, he's crazy—was. I was living with him for God's sakes—on his boat. He just didn't want to take any responsibility. Said *I* should have used protection. Then he bugged me to get an abortion." She shook her head.

"What do you think happened to him?"

"I don't know. He disappeared. If he's dead or in hiding, I just don't know."

"What's your preference?"

She gave a little nervous laugh, but no answer. "All I know is that last night—before he disappeared, I was drugged."

"You sure?"

"No doubt. I know drugs, believe me," she

rolled her eyes again. She was good at it.

"Do you remember who cooked that night?"

"Sure I do. Kay did."

"She says she thinks *you* cooked that night."

"Not me. I'm certain of it."

"Do you think she put something in the food—a drug?"

"That I don't know. Somebody did. I didn't see anyone messing with the food, but I wasn't looking either."

"Anybody say anything about it to you?"

"No. Nobody watched the cooking."

"Any theories on who? Or why?"

"Lots of theories. Think about it often. Used to think about it *all* the time."

"So, who'd want to kill him?"

"Everybody. Me—Kay—Ruth—Elizabeth—Prud-ence—all of us had sufficient reasons for justifi-able homicide."

"What were they?"

"Basically how he treated us. Kay thought he was going to marry her, but it turned out he wasn't. By rights, he should have married me—at least not been such a bastard about our baby. Prudence was out of joint because he didn't favor her. Ruth was incensed at his insensitivity."

"And Elizabeth?"

"Oh, she's another matter. I don't know what her beef was. She just couldn't stand him. She's the only one who talked to me about killing him. But I think she was some kind of gangster or something. To hear her talk, there was always someone from the law breathing down her neck. She talked like she could pop him without giving it a second thought."

"So, if you had to pick one as most likely, which would it be?"

"I was the most hurt," she said. "Oh, maybe Kay thought she was, but I had the baby. All she had was the promise."

"Would you have wanted to marry him?"

"In hindsight, no. But I was in love with him then."

"What about the others?"

"Ruth was mad, but too holy to kill. Prudence didn't have the strength or stamina. She was too la-di-da to get her hands dirty. Elizabeth could have done it, but she didn't care enough. Kay was tough. My money was on Kay—but still I didn't see her as a killer. A husband and kids? Why?"

"So, who does that leave?" I asked. We both knew the answer.

She laughed as her son came off her breast, with no effort on her part to hide it.

My little Plymouth was getting a good workout up and down the coast of Southern California. Returning to L.A., I continually tried to make contact by phone with Ruth to no avail.

I tried a direct approach with Elizabeth. I called her and told her the truth. I had a hunch she might have been in on the murder, or at least privy to it, so I thought I could get a fix on her by being blunt.

"Elizabeth," I said, careful not to call her Liz, Diz, Betty, Petty, Betsy, pesty.

"Yes..." she said, as though trying to place my voice.

"This is Gil Yates. I've been hired to investigate the murder of Les Quincy."

"Oh," she said. Then added in a disconnected tone, "Did they find his body?"

"No. Do you think he might still be alive?"

"Hard to tell," she said. "With him, anything is possible."

I made an appointment to see her on Saturday morning. Tyranny had a show of her adorable figurines in Albuquerque, New Mexico, so the timing was salubrious. My dream was to have Tyranny display her glasswares in some venue with such intense heat they all melted. Elizabeth tried halfheartedly to dissuade me, saying she really had nothing to contribute—the police had already gone over everything with all of them, but I let her think it was an act of Christian charity to see me.

"Gag me," she said to that. "You want Christian charity, you see Ruth."

"You know where she is?"

"No, and I don't want to."

Sunshine was the thing we bragged about in Southern California and we had it in clubs as I drove south on the 405 to Mission Beach on the outpetticoats of San Diego.

The front lawn of Elizabeth's digs was just as nature had intended. Untouched by human hands.

The house was a crackerbox; the curtains were closed.

It was some time before my knock was answered. I thought I saw someone peek out of the curtains, and I heard a hubbub inside. Elizabeth wasn't alone.

When the door opened, I saw the extra time had not been spent tidying up the place.

"Oh, hi," she said, through her handicapped adenoids. "Excuse the mess. The landlord doesn't do anything."

I smiled. I couldn't make sense of that comment. Surely the landlord wasn't responsible for picking up newspapers and magazines, empty beer bottles and half-eaten Big Macs.

Elizabeth may have kept house like my daughter, but there the similarity ended. Her brownish hair was cut short, her face was shoeleather tough, the result of mixing two incompatible races. Irish-American with some South Pacific seasoning in the mix.

Elizabeth was workout trim with clothes that knew their own minds. They stayed very close to home, highlighting all her assets—gems that were not lost on Les Quincy, I was sure.

Elizabeth seemed on edge as I asked my questions. There was a shuffling of feet from the rear of the hovel and Elizabeth's eyes darted in that direction, then to the front when she heard noise there.

"So, what did you make of the trip on the Pacific with Les Quincy?"

"It was the pits," she said, using the vernacular of her high school. "Les Quincy?" she asked rhetorically, and plunged both thumbs down, way down. "A real scumbag."

"How about your fellow crew members?"

"Not too crazy about any of them, either. The whole thing was a sex trip for Les. We worked our butts off running the ship and the almighty captain lounged around with his lady of the night. That was the privileged time for us."

"Any jealousy?"

"You bet!" she said, nodding with vim and vinegar, "nothing but."

"Were you jealous?"

"Maybe a little at first. But then I realized this crazy captain was nothing to fight over."

"Didn't the others?"

"Well, Ruth held out till the end. I think Ruth

could have killed him."

"Why?"

"She was so damn mad at him. He kept after her—digging her for not sleeping with him, ridiculing her religion, her chastity, you name it. Don't get me wrong, I'm no friend of Ruth's, but she got a raw deal."

"How so?"

"He turned on the charm. Ruth was an innocent from some back-woods Bible Belt swamp, and here is the big creep turning on the charm."

"He could *do* that?"

"Well, yeah, he could. And did. You'd have to see it to believe it. He was a babe—a hunk, you know. Every woman's fantasy. He had a smile that could take your breath away—a chest that sent your heart heaving so that you thought it was going to go overboard with you. Why, at certain times, we couldn't wait for our turn. I mean, this is nothing I'm proud of. I'm sure the rest aren't either, that's just the way it was.

"But Ruth was so naïve she got the idea he really cared for her. That's a tough nut for a girl alone to take. She was pining away for this loser in the Bible swamp and he wasn't reciprocating. So, you could say Les was a rebound. Anyway, after Les got her in the sack, he treated her like dirt again. She was broken. Her spirit was on the bottom of the ocean. My heart went out to her. The rest of us were tough enough to take or leave his crap. So he picked on Ruth." She shook her head sadly.

"Do you really think she could have killed him?"

"Yeah—spiritually. I mean, she wanted to, but she wouldn't know how to go about it."

"Anybody else want to kill him?"

"You know, when the chips were down, I think the consensus was to shoot out his knee caps. Ending it for him seemed too humane."

There was more movement in the back of the house. I heard a door open and footsteps going out. The sounds seemed to scare Elizabeth.

"Hey, I'm sure we all wanted to kill him at one time or another," she said.

"Talk about it to anyone?"

She shrugged. "May have."

"What did you talk about?"

"Oh, nothing specific. General stuff."

"Did you do it?"

"Not me."

"Who?"

"You got me."

"No idea?"

"None. Suppose he could have jumped overboard for a swim and a shark got him."

"In the middle of the night?"

She shrugged. "Picked up by another boat in an elaborate scheme to change his identity. Any change he made would definitely be for the better."

"Do you know how Les Quincy was able to afford to go on these trips?"

"I wondered about that. He said he was a flagpole painter and that was good money, but it wasn't *that* good. I think he was getting it somewhere else."

"His wife?"

"Puh," she spit inadvertently. "Not the way he talked. They were *estranged*. Not on good terms at all. I can't see her feeding his libidinous appetites from

Santa Fe. Why would she?"

"To get him out of the house?"

She shook her head. "Easier and cheaper ways to do that," she said.

"Think he could have been transporting some illegal substances on his ship?"

"What?" she said, startled. She seemed concerned now about noises in the back room.

"Drugs and stuff?" I said.

"I don't know," she said. "Could he do that without our knowing it?"

"Maybe that's why you all slept so soundly. Think of it. He's making buys and sales—a wholesaler, say. So he needs you all out of it. Puts something in the lemonade or something. Someone pulls alongside and he does his deal. Only this night, maybe someone was unhappy about a short delivery, or nonpayment or whatever and the next thing Les Quincy knew he was swimming with the sharks."

Elizabeth seemed unaccountably nervous. The activity in back seemed to be increasing.

Suddenly a windy, whooshing sound engulfed the house and I looked outside to see a low-flying helicopter and a half-dozen police cars pointing their menacing grills toward the little house. Two uniformed police jumped out of their cars, guns drawn—and, shielded behind their open doors, they pointed their guns at the house.

I didn't see it at the time, but I heard a scuffle out back that was over in seconds—a like-sized posse had approached the house from the rear and taken down two young males.

Now someone bullhorned us—"Come out with

your hands up. Slowly walk toward the nearest police car. You won't be hurt."

I looked at Elizabeth. I thought I was entitled to some explanation, but I saw only blankness on her face.

Carefully I rose from the chair and waited for her to make a move. She was frozen immobile. "You first," I said.

She looked at me as though I were a Martian speaking his native tongue. Then something seemed to click and her eyes turned alert. They darted about as though looking for a way out.

"Care to sport me to an explanation?" I asked.

She seemed to consider the proposition, then said, "I'm as much in the dark as you are."

The bullhorn sounded its second call to action.

"You lead the way," I said, putting my hands over my head for practice.

She looked at me a long moment, then pushed herself to her feet as though it were a terrible nuisance. "I think you should go first," she said. "You're the man of the house."

"I'm what? It's *your* house. I'm an innocent bystander."

"I'm sure the cops will be delighted to hear that."

A third supplication from the amplified men in blue, this time promising to come and get us if we didn't lean toward the surrender option.

Suddenly, I felt cold and clammy, and a glance at Elizabeth was enough to tell me she shared the terror.

"Come on," I said, "ladies before gentlemen."

She looked at me with a confused look, as though she were trying to determine which was which.

"I know," she said. "You put your arm around my neck from behind—push your fist into my back as though you have a gun. Ask for safe haven somewhere or you'll shoot me."

"No thanks," I said. "They'd have a million excuses to shoot us both."

"You want me to go first? It's like I'm a hostage anyway."

The bullhorn sounded again—"We're coming in."

I threw open the door, and took Elizabeth's wrist and pulled her toward me. I was determined not to stop the first bullet if she pulled any funny stuff.

"You first," I reiterated. "This is *your* game."

I pulled her out in front. "Thanks, stud," she said, with a snort of venom.

We went out, hands high, to face the music.

It was quite a little experience looking down the barrels of all those guns as though I were public enemy number one and the law enforcers were itching to save the state the cost of a trial.

Consequently I was afraid to even breathe, let alone voice my protestations of innocence.

Elizabeth harbored no such reticence, however, and she was vocalizing right up there with a top opera diva. I realized too late the cops must have thought I was the guilty party.

They certainly acted like it when they threw me into an airless, windowless cage at the station house where, after a prolonged cooling period, the good cop and the bad cop took turns grilling me.

The thought that Tyranny Rex and Daddydandruff would miss me before long did not escape me entirely.

"You're in deep doo-doo, pal," the bad cop said. He had a short-sleeved shirt, heavy, hairy arms and dirty fingernails.

The good cop was dressed to the eights—white

shirt, plain-blue tie, sport jacket with a racetrack plaid that made him look like one of Damon Runyon's intimates. His fingernails looked like they had been manicured.

"Going around with an alias doesn't warm the hearts of San Diego's finest," the good guy said, "especially one we can't trace."

It does me no credit that my macho bluffing mechanism was out to lunch. Even the good cop gave me the heebie-jeebies.

"What is it you suspect me of?" I asked, rather meekly, I thought.

Wham! The ham hand of Old Fat Arms pounded the table between us. "Damn it, you know damn well what you were in the middle of down there, and it'll go a lot easier on you if you'll just spill your guts like a good little boy. You'll be happier; we'll be happier."

"Hold on a minute," said the good cop, putting his arm on a flabby bicep of the dog heavy. "Mr. Yates, a.k.a. Something Else, hasn't really given us a good accounting of his side. Why don't we let him tell us who he really is and what he's doing here?"

It didn't take me long to spill my guts. Somewhere, perhaps from my dear mother, I picked up the idea honesty was the best insurance policy. So, I told them the whole bloody thing. When I finished, the cop shook with gales of laughter.

"*You*?" he said. "*You?* Gimme a break. Who the hell would hire *you* to investigate a flea circus?" Wham! The hand again. "What're you hiding? I don't mind keeping you here till hell freezes over if that's what you want. But we want the truth. What's your part in this operation?"

"What operation?"

The hand again. Wham! If he was trying to give me the rubber-hose treatment without laying an illegal hand on me, it was fairly effective.

"You know damn well *what* operation."

I shook my head.

Wham!

"Look," I said. "Why don't you just ask Elizabeth what I was doing there? I don't get this intimidation *schtick*. I know nothing."

Ham Hocks put both hands against the table and pushed his chair back. "I'm outta here," he said. "Let him rot." And he was gone.

My palsy-walsy cop said, "So what do you want to do?"

"I want to get out of here."

"A snap," he said. "I don't believe you were in with those scumbags and their drug operation—but you were in the wrong place at the wrong time."

"Exactly!"

He shook his head sadly. "But we gotta do our job," he said, as though adding, I hope you'll forgive us. He stood up. "Let me talk to your girlfriend—I'll get back to you," and he turned to walk out, leaving me to stew in the soup. I'd read about these games. Sweat a confession out of poor sap by abandoning him for hours in a box—like this one.

"Wait a minute," I said.

He turned, halfway back to me.

"She's not my girlfriend. I never laid eyes on her before today. What's going to happen here? Do I get to call a lawyer?"

"Let me talk to Elizabeth," he said, and left.

In this slammer, I had some terrible thoughts, which I hope will be forgiven me. Like I had ignorantly, by accident, hit too close to the bone with Elizabeth and my drug talk, and Elizabeth was part of it. Perhaps Les learned of her drug connection and wanted to cash in on it—she would have been in the thick of things and now that she thought I'd discovered it, she was this minute selling me out to the cops.

I was left to wallow in my innocence, which they construed as guilt. Their thinking was obviously to sweat a confession out of me.

Fat chance. In all my readings about people in this fix, I never could understand why anyone would falsely plead to unfounded charges.

Sometimes, we live without learning.

The good cop returned and I could see by his face he felt my pain, and he was not the bearer of any glad tidings.

He pulled up a chair. I stood. It seemed to startle him. "Sit down," he said, solicitous of my welfare. "Make yourself comfortable."

"I am comfortable. You left me sitting so long I have saddle sores."

He consulted his watch and seemed surprised. "Time flies," he said. "So, the situation is we know everything. Elizabeth has spilled the beans."

"Great!" I exalted, "then I can get out of here."

He studied my genuine face and after a few telegraphing moments, eternities that told me again the tidings weren't glad—shook his head.

"No such luck, Malvin," he said. "She's pretty much laid out chapter and verse."

"Why...?" I asked, and cut myself off. I knew why.

"The magic of immunity," he said. "You understand immunity, don't you?"

I nodded, dumbly.

"Like to have some?"

I shook my head once, tersely. "Nothing to be immune from. I've done nothing; I know nothing."

His head bobbed as if on a rubber band. "Just a regular guy, a property manager, I believe (he said this with an inflection that said he *didn't* believe). Got any property down here?"

"No. I told you..."

"Little far from home, aren't you?"

"A hundred miles is far these days? Is it against the law?"

"Not if you can explain what you were doing."

"I did."

"Believably," he said. "Look, Malvin, I've known hundreds of P.I.s in my time. It's my line of work. And if I know anything, you aren't it. Now, for everybody's sake—yours most of all—why don't you come clean?"

We did the if-you-are-going-to-accuse-me-of-a-crime-get-me-a-lawyer dance.

"She's laid it all out, Malvin. They do this kind of thing to save their own skins." He shook his head to let me know just how sad he thought the whole business was.

"If she implicated me in any crime, she lied. I don't suppose you will let me see..."

"It's being prepared now. Look, Malvin, I'm trying to help you. I'm going off duty in a few minutes and my partner's coming back. He has lots less patience than I—but I suspect you remember that."

I went over to the table where good cop sat, dejected at my recalcitrance. I put my hands on the table, leaned over on them and turned my face toward his. We were inches apart. "I know nothing about anything those people were doing. If you think I'm an unlikely P.I., where does that put me as a drug dealer?"

"Look, I know you were in on it."

"How do you know that?"

He looked at me as though I were pulling his chain. "Want the secret? I'll give you one—when I finally introduced the word drugs into the mix, you didn't flinch. All along you claimed you didn't know anything about anything."

"That's true. But you let me stew in here a long time. I didn't see what else it could be. Besides after this dull routine, nothing would surprise me."

"Well, Malvin, I want to let you out of here, believe me. I know you aren't the kingpin. Think about immunity—telling us all you know about the big guys in exchange for letting you off the hook, what*ever* your involvement."

"I have *no* involvement," I yelped.

He looked at me a long time. "So you say, pal, so you say." He was clear of the chair and was unlocking the door. "I'll get back to you," he said, and my bleating protests went unanswered.

With maximum invasion of privacy, a guard allowed me to go to the bathroom in his company. I was given the public-enemy-number-one treatment all around.

All my inquiries received the freeze-out treatment. A sandwich of green meat and black cheese was brought to me after dark. It tasted as if it had been assembled in Mexico during the Viva Zapata regime.

Sweetheart with the fat arms came back in. I almost said I thought you were off for the day, but I decided not to give him the satisfaction. I didn't have to—

"Well, Malvin, I would have been gone from here, but you intrigue me. So, let's start from the beginning."

I just stared at him. It was my turn to freeze them out. He didn't seem to pick it up right away. Then after a few more questions, he caught on. "Oh," he said. "I get it." He tried the slamming his ham hand on the table, but I was ready for it and didn't flinch.

More Gil Yates than Malvin Stark, I stared him

down. He didn't know what to make of it.

"Better cooperate Malvin, Boy, or things could go a lot rougher."

"Rubber hose?" I asked.

He eyed me through veritable slits. "Stranger things have happened..."

"I'm sure," I said, not wavering my gaze. "I have answered all your questions honestly. I will not answer any more without an attorney present."

"Oh, that's the way it's going to be, is it?" he mocked me. "You'll be calling the shots, will you?" The hand seemed to be poised for another slam, then he caught himself, perhaps remembering he had already overdone it beyond its effectiveness. "Want to rot here, do you?"

"Look, you bully," I said. "I know the citizens of this lovely country have some minimal rights in situations like this. And you know it too. You guys want another lawsuit, I may be the guy to give it to you."

His laugh was like a burp. "*You?*" he tried to make it sound impossible. "Who would miss Gil Yates? Nobody's ever heard of him, not even Malvin Stark's wife."

"Then I'll be in the clear," I said levelly.

He jumped up as though his seat had heated up suddenly.

"I'm outta here," he said, and he was.

I knew what was coming. An interminable wait and then the good cop again.

It happened pretty much that way. But he brought me Elizabeth's signed statement that I was a drug supplier from Los Angeles. There wasn't a nod of truth in the whole scenario.

After I read it, I handed it back to him with what I hoped was a sardonic smile.

"So, you see, Malvin, it doesn't look good."

"Lawyer," I said.

"I don't blame you. I guess the light bulb has gone on in that head."

"Every word of that is false."

"So, you know about the other two guys? The guys we picked up in back of her place?"

"I do not. I never *saw* them. Every word that refers to me is false."

He looked genuinely disappointed. He heard a sigh across the room. "That's all you have to say?"

"Lawyer," I said.

"I mean, this is going to look pretty good for our side in any court. You recognize her signature, don't you?"

"I do not. I never saw her write anything. Lawyer."

He nodded dolefully, as though I had let him down.

While I was alone, I had time to consider the Tyranny Rex threat. She wasn't home, so I doubted the police had talked to her. But I didn't doubt they'd put a message on her machine that the San Diego Police were holding her husband on suspicion of drug dealing—or worse.

No doubt she would start to connect all those palms and cycads with a windfall from drug dealing. Perhaps, it was time to go public with Gil Yates, I thought. Tyranny Rex couldn't keep a secret to save the spiritual part of her nature.

And Daddybucks? If he ever got wind of my

sideline, I wouldn't have to make any decisions about enduring his abuse. I'd be out with a pratfall. That would be a blessing the mixture of which I could not grasp. I'd always felt my detective work was an occasional sideline that required some gainful employment to fall on. But word had spread and I was getting busy. Jobs were coming my way so I could make as much on one job as I made in six years grubbing for Daddybucks.

But when I was back as Malvin Stark, doubt gripped me in the solar plexus. What if the last job were *the last*?

When I was Gil Yates, I thought since I was the sole support of Daddy Pimple's only daughter, he would be obliged to take me back, should he throw me out on my tail.

But as Malvin Stark, I didn't have that confidence.

In stir, I had time to think about how to waltz around the Wemples. I also had time to fret about the case, which put me in this coleslaw in the first place.

If Elizabeth was running drugs, or running with those who did, was Les Quincy an associate? Or maybe Les was in it all the time. Maybe he even introduced Elizabeth to the trade.

Did Elizabeth really sign that tirade against me? Would such useless information save her hide?

From the cage, the guard moved me to a cell I shared with a drunk who had passed out and one who hadn't. The latter liked to talk but had nothing to say. As far as the wretched smell went, the nose is mightier than the pen.

As the night wore on, an assortment of nature's

mistakes were added to our company, one by one. Each brought with him his own particular malodor. It seemed the larger the mistake, the more likely he was to land up in my cell. I don't think it was a coincidence.

In the morning, they were released one by one until I was the only one left. Obviously, they were playing with me, but I didn't know how to break through the bars and overcome all those armed cops. Most people in my position settle for the status quorum.

A bowl of gruel was served me for breakfast by an uncommunicative guard. All the other prisoners were gone by then. I didn't see anyone until past lunchtime. I kept expecting another green ham sandwich but nothing came.

Around 1:30 p.m. the good cop sauntered in with a half-fried smile on his face.

"Good news," he said. "You're outta here."

I opened my mouth to ask to what I owed this humane treatment, then shut it just as quickly. I had learned at last not to look a gift jackass in the mouth.

At the desk a bored officer returned my earthly belongings and asked me to sign an innocuous looking paper. Fortunately, I read it.

It said, among other things, that I had not been mistreated in my captivity, was read my rights, offered an attorney, free if I couldn't afford one, and I wouldn't file any actions, criminal or civil, against the police.

The good cop was standing over my shoulder to see that I signed it. I looked at him. The cooking smile still pasted there between his nose and his chin. He shook his head. "Sign or stay."

"Hey, you've changed roles with the ugly guy?"

"Sorry, Fred couldn't be with us today..."

"What can you hold me for?"

"We'll think of something," he said, not unfriendly.

And I knew he would. So, I took the ballpoint in my non-writing hand and made a squiggle. Since he didn't ever see my signature as Gil Yates—he couldn't make too much fuss—and I blew him a kiss goodbye.

He gave me the finger.

I was never so happy to turn my back on a guy in my life.

I found myself on the street without transportation. The sports in the station house were all cardiac muscle.

A taxi obliged me and I got to my car, parked in front of Elizabeth's place. A quick inventory told me all the tires were intact. Irrationally, I went to the door of her house and knocked. No answer. I decided not to push my luck. I got in the car and headed north. Perhaps they kept Elizabeth in the slammer. Perhaps her "confession" had been made up.

My first thought was food. The fare at Chez Bastille did little to slake my appetite. So, I drove into the nearest food dispensary, parked the car and just as I got to the cafe door, the ground under me trembled and I felt an earth-shaking explosion that cracked my eardrums in two. I reeled around to look at the source of the pandemonium.

There were a few shards and an engine left where my car had been.

I didn't look back. My heart didn't stop pounding for hours. When it did, and only then, did I think about the ramifications. *Numero uno*—someone wanted me out of the picture. *Dos*—I had a car problem. I needed one. Had it been a more recent vintage, I might have been able to rent one and no one would have been the wiser. The only hope I had for replacing that clunker was to visit the junkyards.

Numero tres—the heap was the property of Daddydandruff of the Elbert A. Wemple Realtors Ass., and I didn't relish that sack of lard asking any questions about how my car blew up in San Diego. But I didn't entertain any delusions that he would let the incident pass unnoticed—because: (1) I wouldn't have a car to do his bidding, and (2) totaled, the value of that car and the insurance payoff wouldn't yield enough to buy a used motor scooter.

Moreover, Daddybucks was intent on strangling the bejesus out of every nickel minted on these shores—as though his miserly stockpiling of U.S. bank notes would save his miserable soul from damnation...but I digress.

I rented a car and drove home. It was the same color as my old one and the same size, but there the similarity ended. I expected to be interrogated by both the Wemples, Daddydollar and Tyrannosaurus Rex Dorcas. (Her close friends call her Dork, and you would too.) So I spent half the drive formulating my responses.

At home, Tyranny Rex was in the garage blowing glass. I used the phone to dance with the insurance company.

"We'll send an adjustor out," said a businesslike lady of a certain age. "Where may we see the car?"

"I'm afraid there's nothing left to see," I said.

"A bad one, huh? Well, we just have to see how bad—even if we call it totaled."

"Well," I said. "Let me ask you what is the totaled value of a Plymouth of that vintage." I gave her the date and listened to her gasp. "Oh, dear," she said. "That was an old one. Perhaps whoever hit it did you a favor."

In a way she was right. When she told me how little it was worth, I decided not to pursue the claim.

The high potentate of Elbert A. Wemple Realtors Ass. was sitting in his elevated cubicle when I stumbled into the factory Monday morning.

"Got a problem," I said mimicking his nibs. *Every*thing was a problem to him, from a two-day vacancy to a grease spot on a carpet.

"Spit it out," he said impatiently, as I helped myself to his exclusive cooled water—"I'm busier than a one-armed paperhanger."

I looked at him in his shiny brown suit with a

pile of dandruff on each shoulder bespeaking a heavy dandruff-day warning to the troops to tread lightly. If my car hadn't blown up in the middle of a case, I would have kept my distance.

"That junker car I've been driving since the Boer War—it blew up."

"What do you mean, blew up?"

"The engine went," I said, not inaccurately.

"So, have it fixed."

"Cost more than it would to replace the car."

"Replace it."

"They don't make them like that anymore."

"Well, tarnation, Boy, do *some*thing, can't you see I'm busy?"

Well, not only couldn't I see he was busy, I've never seen him busy, and his attempts at looking busy entail shifting papers from one side of his desk to the other, and sputtering. He was a world-class sputterer.

But I took him at his word and went out and bought a Dodge Viper (the sporty thing with no top) for seventy grand. I always pay full price when it's on the pimple's tab.

Ha ha. Just kidding. That would have suited Gil Yates to an S or a U or something around there, but Malvin Stark was of a humbler ilk. I went pretty far down the line, but not rock bottom. *And* I got a radio and air conditioning. A first for a Wemple Ass. company car. I knew he'd squeal, and I'd have to listen to that story again about how he was forty years old before he had a radio in his car. To which I wanted to respond that the car radio wasn't invented until he was forty—but I didn't. I'm sensitive to his feelings.

"Air conditioning," he boomed when he looked

at the bill. “I was fifty years old before I had a car with air conditioning.”

I shrugged. “Couldn’t get one without,” I said.

“That’s what they want you to believe, Malvin—you just turn your back and walk out and they’ll come running after you with a car without air—any color you want.”

I clucked my tongue. “I never was the sharp negotiator you are.” I said.

“Damn straight!” he said pounding his palm on his desk, not unlike a certain policeman of my recent acquaintance. “I sometimes wonder what would have become of you if I hadn’t made such a successful ship for you to climb aboard.”

“I’m so grateful,” I said, with sarcasm you could cut with a nail clipper, but he lapped it up as his due.

“What are we going to do about this car?”

I shrugged. “You’re the boss,” I said knowing full well we could no more return a car you’ve driven off the lot than we can put toothpaste back in the tube.

“Did you get a good trade-in?”

“No trade-in. The thing was—”

“No trade-in?” he fumed so, I thought his top would blow, smothering us all in a dandruff blizzard.

“The thing was literally in pieces,” I said.

“Scrap value?” he asked, like a hungry urchin begging for one more bowl of gruel.

I shook my head. “Had almost 300,000 miles on it,” I said, “and it literally blew to pieces.”

“I don’t believe it,” he said, and I didn’t argue. How could I?

The thing about Daddydandruff was if you argued with him, he could go on forever. If you stood there looking dumb—an art, if I may modestly say, I had perfected under his tutelage—he quickly wore down.

So, I had my new car without ever really explaining what happened to the old one.

Tyranny Rex never even noticed the change.

In the meantime, Elizabeth shot to the top of the list of suspects. Whoever set the bomb set it ticking so it would go off after I was some distance from where the bomb had been planted. Fortunately for me, they hadn't factored in my stopping for lunch.

Evil as the bad cop seemed, I didn't figure him for a bomb planter. I thought it *had* to be Elizabeth, or one of her chums, though I couldn't figure why. If I had unearthed some incriminating secret, I couldn't tell what it was.

Perhaps Ruth Waters would provide the key—if only I could find her.

Ruth! It took me a week of digging, but I finally dug her up, as they say in the vernacular.

If you want to find a tennis addict, look on the tennis courts. So, I canvassed the fundamental Christian churches—by phone, with my insurance claim schtick. I could feel the saliva coursing down the dewlaps as as the church rep on the phone who just couldn't give out that kind of information saw a large chunk of the dough flowing into the congregation coffers.

Round-faced, full-breasted, wide-rumped, Ruth Waters cut an imposing figure in the small living room of the digs she shared with her sister in Manhattan Beach—right under my nose.

The house had been built in the boom after our popular war. Walls and a roof were the order of the day.

Ruth was the only member of the crew whose voice rose above the level of indifference when I told her I'd like to talk to her.

"I'd enjoy that," she said. Proof of innocence? Or guilt?

But when I arrived to a greeting of a warm, shy smile I knew she wasn't putting me on.

She was dressed in a blue, velvety mini dress with dark blue panty hose. She wore shoes that might have been referred to as pumps by an observer who knew shoes from asparagus (not I). She had filled out some since she sent the picture of herself into Les Quincy. But she was still a woman to be reckoned with.

She invited me in and bade me sit on the modest couch. She on a straight-backed chair facing me. It had all the fringe benefits of a hair shirt without the itch. Her smile never took a holiday, and she started her story easily.

"No, I never liked him. It was just an impulse thing, really," she said, as relaxed as a goldfish in a bowl with no place to go. "I was *very* religious all my life—praying to God for a better body—weight going up and down like a yo-yo. I got through Bible College and began to wonder what I was going to do with the rest of my life. I realized suddenly I didn't have a clue.

"This crazy opportunity came up. I sent a picture. I got an interview. I sent my resume on Bible College stationery so he would know what to expect. I never thought I'd be picked, because when he asked for a picture I had a good idea what he was after.

"He did some interviews in L.A. so I scraped together the money to fly out. I figured it was a good excuse to visit my sister.

"I was a lot thinner then, but I never considered myself a bathing beauty or anything, and he was all full of himself in the interview and he didn't try to hide what he had in mind. I told him I was chaste and I wouldn't be interested in what he was suggesting.

"I knew I wouldn't be picked—but the next day he called me here at my sister's and told me he had picked the crew and I was on it if I wanted to be. I reminded him of my deep religious beliefs and he said he understood perfectly and he still wanted me. I'll never forget what he said. He said, 'Maybe you'll convert me…or vice versa.' Well, I didn't like the way he said it. I mean, the tone in his voice, you know. So, I told him I'd have to think about it.

"He gave me till the next day at noon. I talked it over with my boyfriend back in Louisiana. He was dead set against it. Went so far as to say if I went he never wanted to see me again. So, I thought that was that. Then I talked to my sister. She's not religious or anything so she had quite a different slant. Called it the opportunity of a lifetime, wouldn't come again—too good to pass up, see the world free—stuff like that. I told her what Mark, my boyfriend, said and she said, 'If that's all he cares for you, you don't want him.'

"He was getting sort of possessive about me, so I decided maybe I'd call his bluff. If he stuck to his guns about it, why, I'd probably be better off without him.

"So, I went. But I guess you know that."

"How was the trip?"

"Terrible. I hated every minute of it. A worse person than Les Quincy I never hope to meet. Miserable."

"What do you think happened to him?"

"I think someone killed him and threw him overboard."

"Who?"

"That's the Final Jeopardy question. The police

couldn't find anything. Nobody, no holes in anyone's story."

"If it was someone on the crew, who would get your vote?"

She shook her head. "'Thou shalt not bear false witness against thy neighbor.' Whoever did it, it was justifiable homicide, and I'm sure God has forgiven her—or them."

"You think it could have been more than one?"

"I don't see how one could have overpowered him."

"Do you remember the last night?"

She shrugged. "Not much different than any other night."

"Sleep well?"

"Always—except..."

"Except what?"

She hung her head and blushed. She didn't say anything.

"I have talked to the others already," I said gently. "I have an idea..."

"No," she said shaking her head. "You have *no* idea, believe me. The humiliation..."

"I'm sure—"

"He was an animal. From day one—once we were out of telephone range of Oahu, he started hitting on me. Oh, he thought it was funny at first, but I didn't and I let him know it. That's what he meant by converting me—he told me his goal was to get me to fall in love with him before the trip was over."

"How long was it supposed to be?"

"Three months or so. 'Well, no way,' I said. It was so crazy. All the others were more beautiful than I was, and they all were willing to do whatever he wanted."

"Ah, but you were the challenge."

"I guess. That wore thin, believe me. Then, suddenly, he changed his approach. He started being real nice. I wouldn't sleep with him and instead of substituting one of the other willing slaves he wouldn't hear of it. 'Your turn is your turn,' he said. 'It's my bed or the deck.' So, it was the deck—rain or shine. He would not let another girl in his bed on my night just to keep the other four bunks full."

"How did the other women take to this kind of life?"

"Like ducks to water," she said. "In no time, it was a regular nudist colony. They thought, what the heck, he's seen us anyway."

"You too?"

"Of course not," she said stoutly, then faltered. "Not...at...first."

I raised an eyebrow.

"You're blushing," she said, as though she had suddenly taken a romantic interest. "No," she said. "He wore me down. I felt so...so defenseless at the time. I really can't even explain it. I was there and there was nowhere—a smallish boat really for six people, ocean all around. Rocking, rocking, rocking all the time, never lets up. It does something to you—hypnotizes you. The sun, the still nights, the sound of the waves on the hull. Then after he'd been so rude, crude and unattractive to me, something inside him snaps and he's Prince Charming all of a sudden."

"How was that?"

"Oh, he made me feel I was the only girl on the

boat—special in his eyes. The others were whores, I was a lady. I had not only a body—we all had bodies—but I had a beautiful soul. At first I thought it was just a line—and I know it was, but you put together all the circumstances and every day I got weaker—just as he knew I would.

"Sooshe was on a trip before—she told me he took a challenge on every voyage and pulled the same routine. It was his little game."

"So, you succumbed?"

She dropped her eyes demurely.

I waited for her to say more. She didn't.

"So, how..." I found myself blushing and unable to complete the sentence.

She looked up now, her expression changing to curious amusement. She tilted her head and studied my face. A wry smile slithered across her delicate lips. She cocked an eyebrow—she stood up and came over to the couch and said, "May I sit here?" with the world of playful seduction in her voice.

I nodded dumbly. She sat beside me, picked up my hand in hers and said, "It was fun while it lasted."

"Do you like sex?" she asked from her intimate vantage on the sofa. We were as close as a razor and a whisker, and I don't have to tell you who was which.

"Well…I…" I faltered.

"Because I do. I used to be all uptight about it and all, and well, I guess I have to give credit where it's due: Les helped me over that hurdle."

I almost fell off the couch. Was she speaking well of the widely hated captain of the ship?

"I thought…" I began.

"Oh, I know," she said. "But I had no experience. I was, like I say, sexually repressed."

"You mean, the guy you lived with…"

"Oh, yeah—Mark. Nothing. We were good Christians, both of us. It was a badge of honor we didn't do anything. That's why he cut me off. He was afraid…what happened would happen, and," she blushed, "well, it did."

"And, it was…okay?"

"Yeah, I have to say…okay. Maybe more than okay."

"But...?"

"But then..."

"Yes?" I prompted her. She seemed to want to leave it at that.

"Then when he was finished having his way with me, he cast me out like a piece of raw hamburger. All that talk of settling down in a cottage by the sea went out the window."

"But...I thought you were mad at him."

Her eyes got a far off, misty look. She moved closer to me until our thighs collided like a knock-kneed Christmas goose.

She turned to look me in the eye. "I wouldn't be mad at you," she purred. Her hand started a startling movement up and down the side of my thigh.

I swallowed hard and tried to bring the focus back to the picture at hand.

"Ruth," I said. "Are you saying now, you didn't want to kill him? All that talk about justifiable homicide was just...talk?"

"Hmm," she said, cozying her head to my shoulder. "I'm not interested in *talk*ing right now..."

There was a sudden flash of warmth between us—like the goose had been liberated and the Christmas cookies were coming out of the oven.

Somehow, we wound up in another room in the house, noted for its horizontal accommodations.

I could imagine what it was like for a woman to take advantage of a man's curious nature to glean information. Those spy stories where the libidinous goddess vamps the unsuspecting grampy with a cache-pot full of state secrets.

But as I got deeper into my intrigue, I developed more admiration for the performers of their craft. For how was one to transfer this romantic energy into semantic synergy?

"Ruth," I protested weakly, "I..." but she covered my mouth with hers.

Ruth had an engaging quality about her. A sweet, almost naïve innocence, that made me want to father her just for a moment. But this was better.

I wish I could tell more, but chivalry is not moribund in my lexicon of etiquette. I can say she was soft and delectable, affectionate in the extreme, but what surprised me more than anything else was there was no talk of white picket fences or solemn commitments.

"I know what you're thinking," she said, as she twisted and turned her clothes to their more or less normal condition. Then she shrugged as if to dismiss the thought.

My dear Dorcas had pretty much shut down in that department after she had the babies. "What's the point of prolonging this messy business?" was, I believe, the charming way she put it.

She had, in other words, done her reproductive duty and since she never got any recreation out of it anyway, that was the law of the land.

Anyone who knew her would have had to agree that was an awful waste of lung power. Of course, meek, mild Malvin Stark just took what he was dished.

But Gil Yates was a different kettle of gefeltefish entirely.

Eager to play to my advantage in an amorous afterglow, I thanked Ruth and asked if she had any theories.

"Not really," she said. "You?"

"I'm beginning to think you *all* did it."

She laughed. "We couldn't even cooperate to cook a meal. How would we plan and carry out a murder?"

"Suicide?"

"Too much ego."

"So?"

"I don't know. I think I heard something, but I don't know what."

"When?"

"That last night. I slept pretty good, but there was some commotion. I remember thinking it odd. Kay was with him and they were making out most of the time, so I thought they were having a terrible argument. Then for some reason I can't explain, I thought of his mother."

"His *mother*? Did you know her?"

She shook her head. "I never met her, but he used to talk to her on the phone and, phew, did he yell at her."

"Could you hear anything from her?"

"Yelling. I could hear it right through the phone. She could yell with the best of them. I remember thinking, he met his match—or maybe he just inherited her temper."

"What were they yelling about?"

"Oh, I don't know. I never paid much attention. It was like 'You did so and so.' 'I did not.' Like school kids."

"How often did you hear this?"

"Couple times. I don't remember. More than once—"

"When?"

"Only when we were near enough to shore to pick up the cell phone signals."

"The first few days?"

"Yeah, maybe. Then, one day at the end when we were getting close and circling the island."

"Circling? Why?"

"That's what he wanted to do. The captain's word is law on a boat. I don't know why we circled. I think it was a kind of perversity. We were all eager to get home, and it was his stupid way of showing us who was boss."

Hm—I wondered. "Did he seem apprehensive—maybe scared of going home—or changing the timing of the landing—or anxious for some reason?"

"Not that I could tell. Kay was his favorite at that point. Maybe she had some feelings. But, wait. Come to think of it, he did seem a little jumpy. At the time I just thought he was being fenced in by Kay, who wanted to marry him. She and Sooshe had awful battles. I mean, there was Sooshe with her pregnancy and Kay with her later claims..." Ruth shook her head at the sad memory.

"Not to mention your own feelings."

"Yeah—pretty much dead by then."

"Did any other boat ever meet your boat?"

"No."

"Could it have happened while you were asleep?"

"I don't know—we slept pretty good."

"Did you have night watches?"

"Sometimes."

"The last night?"

"I don't know. Maybe Les. That would explain why no one saw him go overboard or whatever he did."

"Could he have been drugged?"

She shrugged. "If someone happened to have enough drugs aboard, wouldn't that indicate—what do they call it—premeditated murder?"

"Yeah."

"I take it your theory is we were all drugged—all but the killer?"

"It's an idea."

"So, wasn't Sooshe the only one who knew him before the trip—or before the interview at least?"

I nodded, hoping she would tell me more.

"Why would she wait so long?" she asked.

"Nerve? Getting up the nerve. It's a big step after all, killing someone. Besides, maybe she wanted the trip to see if she could win him back. When she saw the end coming and she hadn't succeeded—wham that's all she inscribed."

Ruth wrinkled her nose. "I wonder why he..."

"What?"

"No, I don't wonder. I was going to say I wonder why Les took Sooshe along again, knowing how she felt."

"So?"

"But I don't wonder," she said. "He was that way. Sadistic."

"So, what's your best guess, Ruth—murder, suicide, accident?"

She thought a moment. "Suicide makes no sense. An accident? We thought about it. The police tried to figure how that could have been possible—the main sail had been stowed for the night so there was no chance of it blowing to knock him unconscious overboard."

"Maybe he tripped on something, hit his head, became unconscious and fell overboard without anyone knowing it?"

"It was a pretty small craft," she said. "If he hit his head hard enough to knock him unconscious, don't you think one of us would have heard something?"

"If you weren't drugged, you mean."

"Well, we certainly wouldn't have had to have been drugged for an accident. Not unless the 'accident' was planned."

"Yeah," I said.

On my way back to the slave quarters in Torrance, California, USA, I tried to make sense of the puzzle. I couldn't. I had talked to them all, and gotten some personal impressions and a lot of inconclusive information.

I had a soft spot for soft Ruth, but that was understandable. Too understandable. I could have easily have been set up to overlook her complicity. As far as the technicalities were concerned, every one of them had some motive for sending their captain to the bottom of the sea.

Oh Captain, my captain, our fearful trip is done.

And yet, I couldn't see any of them making the final push. I was fairly convinced there had been some drugging in the rigging, but not thoroughly convinced. They all spoke of how tired they were at the end of the day. So, I had convinced myself that the death occurred because of some peripheral issue. Drug running is always a good bet. That would implicate Elizabeth and the nice person who bombed my car. A woman scorned? Sooshe, Kay, Ruth maybe even Prudence. The hometown folk tried to keep me away from Prudence.

Maybe there was more to that.

Why would the folks in Tennessee and San Diego want to do me harm if there was no complicity? But if I had to choose the *least* likely murderess, I'd choose Prudence. She seemed most immune to Les Quincy's charms.

The dogs were barking up the wrong timber.

But, so far, it was nothing but hunches. If I had any hope of earning my fee—or annuity might be more like it—I'd have to get something in asphalt. One of those hard things they make roads out of. All I had was fluff. And a lot of expenses.

Tyranny Rex was not at home, and that was always a blessing.

I called Les Quincy's widow, Edna.

After the exchange of a few pleasantries, and a cursory report on my progress, I asked, "What can you tell me about Les's mother?"

There was a rocky silence. "We don't get along," she said at last. "I didn't see her much."

"How did Les get along with her?"

"Not well."

"Can you tell me more?"

"Not really. Les spent a lot of time in Honolulu. That's where she lived. She was jealous of me. The classic mother-in-law syndrome, I guess. I was younger, prettier, her son liked me better. She saw me as a replacement, I guess. Didn't like it."

Edna sounded a little defensive to me. She was arguing a case that I didn't ask to have argued.

"So, what was their relationship in Honolulu?"

"She was religious to a fault. He rebelled. Did things she didn't like. So I guess you'd say their relationship was strained at best."

"Yet he chose to stay there between trips—rather than coming back to Santa Fe?"

"Well, it was just easier and cheaper. In that one case, I mean. He used to come back here. But he was planning a South Pacific Island fling in a few months so it didn't make a lot of sense for him to come back here."

"Not even to see his wife?" I said to another shut out. I heard a sniffle, then a heavy exhalation. I decided I could live without that answer. It was self-evident anyway.

"Did you ever call him on the ship?"

"Sure."

"What did you talk about?"

"I don't know. Nothing special. Things."

"Argue at all?"

"Oh, I suppose we argued like most people."

"Remember what about?"

"Small stuff—I can't remember now."

I didn't like the way this conversation was going. I thought she was hiding something. Maybe a lot of things. The contrast between my first meeting and this one couldn't have been greater.

"Are you alone there?" I asked out of the teal.

"Yes," she said, but for some reason I didn't believe her.

"Do you have a name and address for Les's mother?"

"Yes—somewhere," she said. "Last name I know of is Hatborough. Ada Hatborough. She's had a few husbands, and the last I knew she was a widow again."

"A widow? Again?"

"Yes, she lost Les's father when Les was growing up—he was about twelve or so as I remember him telling me. Then she remarried and lost that one too."

"How did he die?"

"I think he had heart problems. Les didn't say much about it. They didn't get along."

"When did he die—before or after the last trip?"

"Oh, before. I think it was between trips. Yes, I remember Les telling me how hard his mother was taking it. I can understand it. We older girls are not in any kind of demand I can notice."

"How long were they married?"

"I'm not sure. Around twenty-five years maybe. Les was in high school."

"What did the husbands do for their living?"

"First one made some money in some kind of real estate. Second was military, I believe."

"Army? Navy?"

"Yeah, Navy, I think. Make a difference?" she asked.

"Never know."

"Oh, here's Ada's address," she said, and read me the number and street in Honolulu.

"Phone?"

She gave me a number.

As soon as I hung up, I realized another Honolulu trip was necessary. Too much mystery about Les's mother. The Widow Quincy had become too strange.

I'd take the Friday night flight to Honolulu without any evasive dancing to appease Tyranny Rex.

She probably wouldn't miss me anyway.

I passed the next few days on idle at the foot of Elbert August Wemple Realtors Ass. I must have looked busy, for except for the usual imagined calamities by the great calamity creator himself, he left me pretty much alone.

When I got home, Tyranny was not about. She isn't about much when you think of it. Glass blowing is about it. I took the opportunity to do a little business.

I called my old pal at the San Diego P.D.

"*Mal*vin!" he said, with his malevolent pronunciation. "You wouldn't believe I was just talking about you with your friend Fred. That was a nasty mishap you had with your car."

"Malfunction."

"I'll say," he said. "We were wondering since you weren't in it and all, maybe it was self-inflicted, if you know what I mean."

"I don't know," I said, "and I don't want to."

"We could pull you back in," he said.

"For bombing my own hundred year-old car?"

"Yeah, whatever."

"It's another no-winner," I said.

"Yeah, we figured."

"So, what can you tell me about those gems you hauled in there when you made your false arrest of me? They in this big time?"

"Well, big is a big word. How big is big?"

"Big enough to blow my car up—a stranger—to shift some blame?"

"Well, that's what we wondered. On the other hand, if you were a known commodity to them—say they saw you as a threat, make it more understandable."

"Me? A threat?"

"Yeah, I know what you mean. But stranger things have happened."

"So, where are you with them?"

"Got 'em locked up. They're just punks—won't sing on the band leader. Scared witless (Well, his word *rhymed* with witless).

"And the girl? Elizabeth?"

"Punk's moll—she's a bit player. Between us, hotshot, we figure she's in it for the male companionship, if you don't put too fine a point on it. No accounting for taste they say. Got to keep her on edge. She can help."

"Any evidence of any contacts, accounts?"

"Such as?"

"Guy named Les Quincy? Elizabeth was on a boat with him for a couple months. He disappeared. Drugs a possibility."

"Thanks for the tip," he said, with a ladle of sarcasm in the pot.

"May I call you later?"

"Hey, I'm a public servant. I am at your service."

If I believed that, I'm sure he had some bridges on which he could make me very good prices.

My next call was to Edna Quincy—this reminder of my blown-up car made me curious about something I had not had the wit to ask about.

"What do you know about Les's boat?" I asked Edna after a minimum of pleasantries.

"It sank," she said, with such a dull thud I thought it was sinking inside her.

"Yes, and I hear his mother got the insurance. Shouldn't you have been the beneficiary?"

"That's what I thought," she said with the song of sadness trailing after her.

"I thought you sponsored this..." I wasn't sure what to call it, "...hobby of your husband's."

"I thought so too," she said. "Apparently, he was working both ends." I heard sniffling on the line.

"I'm sorry," I said.

In a moment the sniffling stopped. "Oh," she said. "No. I was just...you know, I didn't even know Les was dead until the people who insured the boat filed a police report. none of those girls even told anyone Les had disappeared."

Why she had stayed loyal to him? I wondered after I hung up the phone.

You'd think all this air travel would calm my flying nerves. You'd think wrong.

For a guy too queasy to even think about suicide, every time I bought a ticket on one of those death machines with wings, I thought of nothing else but a sudden end to it all. Very sudden.

The flight was, as usual, eventful. Some oaf bumped into a flight attendant, whose first flight was with the Wright brothers. She dutifully spilled a tray of boozy drinks on my pants. The upside was her wiping action was quite sensual, took my mind off the inherent dangers of being suspended in midair over the largest, most enormous and forbidding ocean in the world. All this in a contraption too heavy by half to stay in midair stuffed full of people stuffing themselves with Satan's leftovers as though they didn't weigh too much already.

Naturally, I called my daughter as soon as I landed in Honolulu. Just as naturally, I was told she was at the library.

"Tell her, her old dad called, please. I'm back in town if she has any interest in a free meal." I left my number at the down-scale hotelry of choice.

After I dumped my minimal portable belongings in the land-view hotel, I walked to the marina docks.

It was like a prize-winning photograph—in glorious color. Ocean, bay, hills, hotels, boats bobbing to and fro on water so clear it looked like you could drink it without getting hepatitis.

For my stroll on the boat dock, I employed my innate homing device to scope out old timers, storehouses of boat lore and gossip.

My mark had a full beard, stained by chewing tobaccy, and blurry eyes beaten by the sun and perhaps repeated doses of under-the-counter pain killers.

"Yeah, I remember old Les," he said, trying to appear blasé but glad of the opportunity to spout off like a sperm whale.

"Know what happened to his boat?"

"Sank," he said, giving me a sinking feeling that was all he was going to say.

"Well, I guess it was insured," I said.

The mouth amid that nicotine-stained beard remained closed. I wasn't sure if it was because he didn't have the information or he didn't want me to have it. I kept staring at him as though that might break the spell.

Finally, he spit some tobaccy on the dock and shook his head. "Funny business, that," he said.

"Yeah? How so?"

"You know about Les," he said, less a question than a courtesy. "A man take his way with alla them girl's bound to have problems."

"Think someone sunk the boat to get back at him?"

"Don't know about the boat, but someone sunk Les himself."

"Any ideas?"

"Nah, coulda been any of 'em, all of 'em, their relatives an' friends. Anybody had it in for Les, an' way I understand it, they was standin' in line."

"Who insures these things?" I asked, waving insouciantly at the bobbing boats moored to the dock.

Though he seemed reluctant to do so, he muttered the name of the *primo* boat insurer in these parts. "Sal Snethkamp, up a ways on the main drag."

I didn't push.

Why do I always think the possessor of an androgynous name is a male? Sal wasn't. She was, well a she—and a well-built she at that. Sal was blonde, young enough, but not untested. She easily could have put me in a testing mood.

She sat in a storefront, two-desk office. The other desk was unoccupied.

There was a potted palm—a *Laccospadix forsteriana* in the corner beside her desk, and a visitor's chair at each desk. No expense was unspared on waiting rooms or other pretensions to wealth.

"Hi," she said, her voice matching the Honolulu sunshine.

"You do boat insurance?" I asked.

"You got a boat?" She must have seen me as an unlikely boat owner.

"If I did?"

"Write you anything you want."

"Do a lot of it, do you?"

She looked askance at me. "Who am I talking to?" she asked.

"Gil Yates," I said, macholike. "Private investigations."

"Oh, oh," she said. "Is my ex trying to catch me in a compromising position?"

"Would that be hard to do?"

She shook her head with a wan smile. "I'm very easily compromised," she said. "Finding a compromiser? Now that's another matter."

I don't remember how long it took me to get over that one. A lot of positions flashed through my mind, compromising and un—with the emphasis on the former.

I glanced at the empty desk. She read my mind. "Dad's desk," she said. "He comes in every couple years. I keep the desk as a shrine. Makes him feel important."

"Les Quincy," I said, getting back on track.

She looked startled. "You aren't Les Quincy?"

"You insured his boat..." I said, copying her inflection.

She paused before she nodded, as if to clear her suspicions that I might be investigating her. "Sucker sank," she said like an old salt.

"Accident?"

She shrugged. "Not like any I've ever seen. Facts were sketchy. One day the boat—" she waved her hand—"pft. Then we find out the skipper had disappeared."

"Foul play?"

"Foul may be an applicable word. Play it wasn't."

"Who got the dough?"

"Mother."

"Yeah? Hatborough?"

"That's her."

"Remember how much?"

"Around two hundred big ones," she said.

"Fight it?"

"For a while. Couldn't get anything. That was a tight bunch. The crew, the family. The crew had pretty much dispersed by the time the boat went down. No one seems to know what happened to Les."

"But the boat. They sank it for insurance didn't they?"

"Well, if you know who 'they' is, I wouldn't mind you sharing the information with yours truly."

"Thought you might have an idea."

"Yeah, I had some ideas—but, as I said, nothing took."

"Anything strike you as peculiar about the policy?"

Sal thought a moment. I had the feeling she was taking her time to make me believe she was giving my request the attention it was due.

"Oh," she said at length, "I guess I don't get many mothers buying the policy. This time the premium was paid just before the boat went out again. And she didn't stint on the valuation."

"A tipoff that something nefarious was afoot?"

"Never know," she said, with a twist of her head. "in this business, you just never know."

"Cops help?"

"Not much. They seem to feel these things are petty civil disputes; we shouldn't bother them with. I have a suspicion the mother only filed the police report because the insurer requires it."

"What do you think?"

"Me, I don't think. I just do my job. I sell insurance. I don't second-guess claims. That's another department."

"Think his mom had it sunk for the payoff?"

"I told you, I don't think. Tends to hurt the business."

"Could it hurt you—physically, I mean?"

She looked at me a long moment, then whispered, "You aren't as dumb as you look."

"How could I be?" I asked and after a second-thought moment, she joined me in a good laugh.

I low-tailed it over to see Ada, Les's mother. The house was on a pleasant street, on a gentle climb. I parked the rental I'd gotten at the airport and went with high-minded purpose to the front door. I rang the bell.

Nothing.

Knocked.

Nothing. Well, that's all part of the game. When you want to surprise someone you often come up with an empty bucket.

My attention turned to the landscape, which was opulent if you were into understatement. Without thinking I might be intruding, I followed a path of plumbago, plumerias, bougainvillea, Brachychiton flame trees, as well as a few tantalizing palms and exquisitely cared-for cycads, with the emphasis on my beloved *Encephalartos.*

As I rounded the corner and came into the backyard, I heard a grunt of displeasure that could have come from a person or an animal. I looked up from the horticultural gems and saw the source of the sound.

She was sitting on an oversized redwood garden bench, turned gray by the elements—both the bench and the formidable woman.

Imperious was the word that came to mind. The kind of mother you hoped was someone else's.

She looked like a Hawaiian overstuffed on breadfruit, but she was really a gringo overfed on the rich culinary luxuries. She wore one of those Hawaiian shirts that shifted when she did, which wasn't very often. But when she did shift in that shirt, the plumbago flowers did a circumspect dance. Around her neck she wore a heavy looking cross with a Jesus figure slumped forward as if just about to fall from his crucified position. Ada, too, leaned forward as though she was about to topple from the weight of her cross.

She reminded me a little too much of Tyranny Rex to generate any meaningful warmth in me; and her unwelcoming glare turned me rockyroad cold.

Her house seemed simple and unpretentious, but her garden was astonishing in its splendor of bloom and lush greenery. Especially gripping were the bountiful palms with gracefully arching fronds offering privacy from the neighbors and protection from the harsher elements.

At kneecap level flowed a sea of cycads of immodest proportions, some of them six feet across. They rendered the offerings in front to midget status. A quick pan around the place with my mind's camera put those cycads, even if a lot of them were common ones, at a hundred grand or more; and here was this *grande dame* on her throne as though monarch of all she surveyed. And she wasn't suffering me gladly.

"Mrs. Hatborough?" I asked tentatively, wanting to make sure I hadn't stumbled on an overfed maid.

She looked at me, this mountain of forced femininity, through a half-cocked eye, as though she were a poker player calling my bluff.

"And who are you, young man, to invade my privacy in this manner? I may be wrong, but I have no recollection of inviting you here."

If she thought she could throw me off balance with that kind of bravado, she didn't know the distaff, Tyranny Rex. I shifted to suckup mode.

"I do hope I'm not bothering you, ma'am. I'm Gil Yates, and I'm investigating the mysterious disappearance of your son, Les Quincy."

She looked right through me. "I know his name," she said. "The memory is an unhappy one for a myriad of reasons I do not care to go into. I'm afraid I will be of no help to you."

"Because you can't" I asked, "...or won't?"

Her gaze shifted slightly to a spot between my eyes, as though she were searching for the perfect place to place a bullet. With one hand she gripped the arm of the bench she was severely straining with her bulk. She pitched forward as though the cross were pulling her. When she was more or less upright I noticed that a massive arm was lifting the bench off the ground. It was the arm of a Sumo wrestler, and it didn't take a rocket scientist to grasp that it shouldn't be trifled with. In a blur of mystical strength she hurled it towards me, and had I not the agility to sidestep, I might have been rendered more or less a pancake.

Her glare in my direction said, "Goodbye."

I took the hint.

Before going back to the hotel to see if there was a message from my daughter, Felicity (hope springs eternal in the human chest). I stopped by the residence of Kay Sagerstrom and her close friend, the Admiral.

Unfortunately, it was the latter who opened the door. His expression was one of perpetual disapproval.

"Hi," I said. "I was in the neighborhood, and I just thought I'd drop in to share my experiences with the crew with Kay." When his silent glare didn't waiver, I added, "I thought she might be interested."

He thought otherwise, for he closed the door in my face. Not a friendly bunch here on the Aloha Islands.

Of course, the Admiral's reaction made me more suspicious that he was protecting his girlfriend.

I waited an indecent interval before ringing the bell again. I heard a heating discussion, man to woman, inside. That would be Kay and the Admiral arguing about me.

The Admiral opened the door, Kay was right behind him. "I told you, sir, your presence is no longer wanted here."

"Honey!" Kay said, "Let him in. He's not doing any harm. We can certainly be more hospitable than that. Besides," she added with a certain seduction in her voice, "he's kinda cute, don't you think?"

"No. I don't," he said emphatically, as if in some defense about a subliminal mention of homosexuality.

"Oh, come on in, Gil. The Admiral thinks I'm a delicate flower, wilting in too much sun—in constant need of rain and fertilization." This last she said with an energetic batting of the eyelids.

The Admiral threw his hands apart as if to say, I wash my hands of the whole mess. He again disappeared somewhere in the house with such alacrity I thought he must have been a submarine commander in his career. One thing I was sure was he was a good man with a torpedo.

"Gosh, it's good to see you again, Gil," she said, her eyes sparkling on mine as though she really meant it. Maybe the old salt wasn't lighting the fires in her heart as she had hoped. I couldn't help but find her manner decidedly flirty.

We settled in side by side on the swing on the back porch facing another stellar Hawaiian garden. She sat so close to me I could feel the warmth of her body radiating off my clothing. I thought if the Admiral saw us, I might be the target of one of his torpedoes.

"So, what did you learn from my shipmates?"

I shrugged as if the answer was nothing of importance. "Everybody has a different take. As someone once said, 'Life is all a matter of perspective.' The consensus was, however, that you did the meal preparations on the last night out."

"Really? I thought it was Sooshe," she shrugged, "but the days and nights did run together somewhat."

"So, it *is* possible?"

"Why not? Does it matter?"

"Well, the other consensus, if there is one, was someone slipped something in the food to put select members to a reliably sound sleep. She or shes who were not affected carried out the deed—probably on a victim who was also drugged."

"Hm? Anyone admit to being awake? To hearing anything?"

"No," I shook my head. "Would you?"

"No, if there was any drugging going on it hit me too."

"Did you hear any fighting on the ship?"

"Oh, nothing serious," she said. "Arguments..."

"About what?"

"Les mostly, I guess."

"Anything on the phone?"

She looked startled. "Phone? Did we have a phone? I don't think..."

"Les had a cell phone—"

"Oh—I never used it," she said as though she weren't sure and if she had used it she shouldn't admit it. Kay was getting more cautious with her answers.

"Did you ever hear Les arguing or shouting on the phone?"

"Not that I remember," she said with a frown. "Why? Did someone else?"

"Maybe—did you know Les's mother?"

"I knew he had one."

"Ever meet her?"

"Where would I—?"

"She lives not far from here."

"That so? Well, it's a small world, isn't it? Let's have a drink, Gil, what do you say?"

"Oh, no thanks."

Her eyelids twinkled. "Afraid I'll take advantage?"

I batted my own lashes, "Easily done," I said.

She looked interested. "I'll keep that in mind," she said.

"Any further thoughts on the, how shall I put it—tragedy?"

"You're the one who talked to everyone. You tell me. What did you learn?"

"All boiled down?"

"Why not—like corned beef and cabbage—one of Les's favorite dishes by the way."

"The night he disappeared, you prepared the last meal. Everyone, with the possible exception of you, was drugged. Evidence would point to you."

"Me? Where would I get the drugs—out of the ocean? How would I know to administer them—? and probably most important—why on earth would I want to kill the man I wanted to marry?"

"Because he didn't want to marry you, maybe?" It was a real question.

"Who said that?" she snapped.

"It was suggested as a possibility," I said non-committally.

"Bunch of jealous bitches," she said. "They *all* wanted him. *I* got him—you have to expect some back-biting, I guess." She seemed to be pondering if she could accept that. "I suppose they were all trying to save their backsides by implicating me, but it's just too preposterous for words—" she paused, then searched my face for a weak spot. "Nothing like this came out with the police."

"Yeah, why not?"

"Because they must see you as more of a threat—"

"Why? Were they all in on it?"

"I don't know. I only know I wasn't."

"Do you remember cooking that last meal, now?"

"Not really."

"What's the last one you remember?"

"I told you. One was much like the other. Oh, this is too ridiculous, Gil. I know nothing of knockout drugs. Where was I supposed to get them?"

"Maybe he had sleeping pills."

"Really? Enough to knock everybody out?"

"I could be wrong, but sleeping pills aren't that unusual. Not knowing what to expect on a little boat on a big ocean, maybe a lot of you had them."

"But I was going to *marry* him."

"You seem to be the only one who thinks so. The only person who can validate that claim isn't around anymore."

She looked at me long and hard, as though that look would make me putty in her hands. It nearly worked, for she was truly a looker.

She put her hand on my knee. "Gil," she said. "This is real silly. I'm attracted to you. Was the moment I laid eyes on you. I like sex. Always have. Can't help it. I'm a pushover for a man. But I make love, not war," she paused to read my reaction. I tried to make it dispassionate. "Want me to prove it?" she said, with those hypnotic eyes.

Her hand began a tantalizing climb to a central location on my defenseless body.

"But...what about...the Admiral?"

"Oh, pooh, he's down below deck as he calls it, getting quietly plastered, an art he has perfected. He's a nice guy—treats me well—within his capabilities. But he's no stud...like you."

"What makes you think...?"

"Don't be modest—all I had to do was look at you," she leaned over and with her hand in high gear, gave me a kiss on my mouth that I was at a loss to resist.

Just then I heard the voice of the U.S. Navy. "Kay—what are you doing?"

He didn't sound very drunk to me.

"We're expected at the Simpson's in five minutes," he said, "are you ready?"

"Randy," she whispered in my ear, "would be more like it—" she tightened her hand and I suppressed a squeal.

"Well, I've got to go, Gil. I've enjoyed our chat immensely. Will you take a rain check?"

I was about to say I would when she said, "How about tomorrow night? We're having a party. A reunion of sorts—"

"A reunion?"

"Yes. All the girls from the crew are coming back for a reunion. Interested?"

I was.

Before things got too involved, I decided to drop by Felicity's place, on the off chance the library was closed.

Closed or not, I found her in the embrace of yet another young man, from whom she disengaged long enough to open the door for me and invited me in with a warmth of hospitality unrivaled by a perturbed Gila monster.

Felicity had been through more men in her time than she had blessed colleges with her presence. It was a tossup from which she had learned most.

Tyranny and I had been blessedly blessed with the acquaintance of only a few of them—such was Felicity's interest in our approval ratings on her young men.

I always wondered, foolishly perhaps, if I would be able to pick Felicity's boyfriends out of a lineup. Like—here Dad, are six guys. Which one—(or I suppose even two) are mine?

It wouldn't necessarily be the scruffiest one, but it probably wouldn't be the neatest, most intellectual looking one of the bunch, either.

Would I have been able to pull Fritz from his peers?

Maybe not. He was neat and clean, no taller than Felicity, as muscular as a gymnast. If his movements were any indication—in a race with a tortoise, I'd bet the tortoise.

She accepted my dinner invitation on condition that Fritz could come along. My children seemed to curry the protection of strangers when dealing with their father.

The place they took me was not reticent about charging, and I was beginning to calculate what this case would cost me if I didn't crack it soon.

A San Francisco brothel in the late 19th Century—that seemed to be the model for the decor of this eatery. Burgundy velvet wallpaper, Tiffany lamps, crushed velvet chairs and couches in the entryway—the same bloody red fabric on the seats and backs of the chairs. It was some entrepreneur's answer to the ahh—loh—*hah* feeling of the open-sided sheds that said welcome to down home Honolulu.

The only feeling I got out of this place was discomfort. Meals in fancy restaurants like this were not in my budget—$11.50 for soup—$32 for a slab of meat, more if you were a vegetable fan—$12 desserts—and I don't have to tell you who among us ordered those. The wine list, of course, read like a price list of late-model used cars.

"So, what's new, Felicity?" I said, trying my tried, if not always true, ice breaker.

"Exams, term papers, spot quizzes, I'm going nuts."

Yeah, I thought. Passing any? but I looked at Fritz and decided against any questions in that line.

"What are you studying, Fritz?" I asked, deciding to give him the benefit of the doubt.

"Bartending," he said, unaffectedly.

That was the thing about Felicity, she chose her friends with an eye to the unthreatening. Fritz, it turned out *was* a bartender. Not just in any old saloon, but for the town's snootiest caterer. I realized I was expected to react to that news as though she had announced he had just been tapped for the Phi Beta Kappa Society.

Then the good news—"Fritz gets me jobs now and then. I'm working tomorrow night at one of his gigs in town."

"Oh, yeah, where?" I said, feigning interest that I didn't have.

She looked at Fritz.

"Some couple in the hills having a party," he said. "An admiral and his bimbo."

Could it be? I guessed this island was fairly crawling with admirals and more than one of them could have a young woman friend who could fairly be characterized as a bimbo and yet, hadn't I been invited to a party sounding suspiciously like this one? Immediately I thought of how I could use them in my service.

"So," I asked Felicity. "What do you do at the party?"

"I'm renting out for the evening with my short skirt and apron. I hold a tray and canapés and flash my rear for the geezers."

"Been to their house before?" I asked Fritz,

embarrassed at my daughter's characterization of her first gainful employment.

"Oh yeah," Fritz said. "They like to give parties."

"What kind of people go?"

"Oh, his Navy buddies—her tennis and golf pals—neighbors, I don't know. Once we did a wake for a friend of the admiral's."

"Yeah? Who died?"

"One of his Navy buddies. Real thick with the Navy stuff—anchors aweigh."

"Know his name?"

"Nah," he said. "Big fat woman was his wife. I remember wondering what he had seen in her. Then I heard she had big bucks."

"How'd you hear that?"

He shrugged. "You hear stuff at those parties. Oh, yeah," Fritz said, turning to Felicity. "Her son was that guy you interviewed for—" then back to me "takes chicks out on his boat."

"Yeah," Felicity said, her mouth half full of lobster thermidor ($33.50), a glass of Chardonnay at hand ($175.00 the bottle), "that was the guy I told you about."

"Yeah," Fritz said. "They weren't too taken with him, I remember."

"Why?"

"Don't know—just their general attitude."

Sometimes you dig so long you finally fall in or as they say, if you're in a hole, stop digging.

The deeper I sank into this *femme fatale* bacchanal, the more my reluctant admiration for Felicity grew. She'd had the good sense to shun this fated trip—or she might have been in this fish soup along with the rest of them.

I wondered what it was that set girls apart in a matter like this. Those who would take a trip like this and those who wouldn't.

Whatever it was (parental guidance?!) I was proud of my girl, though it was indicative of our relationship that I would probably never be able to tell her so.

That night, back in my unconsoling hotel room, I thought of ways Felicity and Fritz could help me without showing my hand. Not that Felicity would tell her mother or grandfather what I was up to—she wasn't that much of a communicator.

I'd often wondered what the reaction would be if Tyranny Rex found out about my secret career. I expect she wouldn't believe it. She would think about it for a minute or two—unless she was preparing for a show—then she just wouldn't have a minute.

Daddybucks Wemple, from his elevated throne room would say something like, "What, are you nuts? Stop dogging it and get back to work. We got a ball of snakes out in Gardena!"

So why bother?

And why worry? I know what they say about worrying. About how ninety percent of the things you worry about never happen, and the other ten percent would have happened whether you worried or not, so why worry?

No why, just do.

So, I formulated a plan. It was more than a windfall to have these two—critters—as extra eyes and ears at the party. If they would cooperate. And after I sported them to a dinner, the tab of which would have bought a nice two bedroom house in some venues, I was counting on the spirit of beholdenness.

But my plan would have to be foolproof. I sat up deep into the night honing my scheme like a steel trap.

The invitation was for 7:00. I got there at 7:03. I didn't want to miss anything.

Kay greeted me like a lost lover who returned in time's old nick. She wore a colorful, Hawaiian print sarong with lots of antheriums and protea flowers on a yellow background. The dress was without imagination. None was needed. Every surface of the house seemed to be holding a mess of flowers—as if a drunken painter had opened all his cans at once.

Kay looked me in the eye and held me in her gaze as though I were the handsomest creature on earth. "Oh, Gil," she said with a warmth that could not be mistaken for mocking, "I'm *so* glad you could come."

Then clasping both my hands in hers, she leaned over and whispered in my ear, "When things settle down a bit, I hope we'll get some time alone together," and her eyes told me she wasn't thinking of tennis.

She led me by the hand out through the back of the house where the entire wall seemed to have magically disappeared.

The yard was lit with hurricane lamps. A seven-piece band was playing that dreamy Hawaiian music sliding all over the place with ukeleles and steel drums.

In the central barbecue pit a pig was roasting on a spit with an apple in his mouth. In case he got hungry, no doubt.

Just inside the house—at the open wall—a table, resplendent with delicacies stretched from wall to wall. There was an expansive bar at the end of the yard—Fritz commanding. A swinging door to the kitchen swung open and my Felicity appeared—as advertised—in a skimpy costume which would make burning Sterno obsolete.

She was carrying a tray of crab cakes, toothpicks for the sticking and transferring of the goods to the mouth, and little napkins for cleaning up the mess.

I stood in front of Felicity, speared a crab cake with a toothpick, took a napkin and in a low voice, laid out my plans for her.

I slipped the one hundred dollar bills discretely into the napkins, one for Felicity, one for Fritz. I told her Daddybucks was considering selling one of his apartment buildings to these people and he had a funny feeling about them. I was being dispatched to "check them out."

I needn't have bothered. Kids that age don't question one hundred dollar bills.

Then I went to Fritz's bar, asked for a bottle of mineral water (far superior to nonmineral water) and made, in the same quiet, offhand manner, my requests, handing him a one hundred dollar bill laden napkin in the process.

"Oh yes, sir," he said with some gusto, "a fine

evening indeed."

There were only a few people there when I arrived, but they were beginning to pour in in more respectable numbers.

I looked around but didn't see any of the all-girl crew yet. Maybe that was just a teaser to get me to come. I didn't need any teasers—Kay was doing a good job of that herself.

Ada Hatborough made her entrance with the aid of a cane. A sturdy silver cane, as it turned out. Around her neck hung the ponderous Jesus on the cross which threw off specks of light and seemed to pull her forward. She was in a black dress which would have flowed had she been lots thinner, but now billowed where she did. Black was definitely her color.

I always wanted to use the word doyenne, and here she was—the perfect stately dowager—doyenne to the tips of her bloated ankles.

She seemed intent on poking holes in the floor beneath her cane wherever she went, so purposefully did she slam it down with every step. I kept my eyes on her and her cane. I remembered the flying bench and I I didn't want that silver rod piercing my heart.

Ada Hatborough made her way straight for the bar, her jackhammer cane preceding her.

She zeroed in on the Admiral who was transacting some intercourse with Fritz. Ada seemed to bawl old Poop Deck out from the first word exchanged. He waved a hand as though passing off some blame to a convenient sprite in the sky.

When they got their drinks, they moved away from the bar. I moved in, thrust out my glass and said audibly, "May I have some more water, please?"

"Yes, sir," Fritz said, then *sotto voce:* "She: 'What is that snoop doing here? Are you out of you mind?' He: 'Tell me about it! It was Kay's idea. She thinks she can charm him.' She: 'I know how she'll charm him...but I have a better idea.' Then they walked away."

"Thanks," I said, when he handed me the water.

Then, as if someone had cued them, the four other crew members made their entrance in concert. It was quite an effect, like reindeer on the roof. But with fillies like these, Santa was superfluous. They seemed even more stunning collectively than they had individually.

Certainly, I was troubled that they had all come so far for this "reunion" so soon after I had just seen them. The girls were all smiles and charm as they made an angry dash for me. Ruth got to me first, then Sooshe and Prudence, and Elizabeth brought up the *derrière.*

"How *are* you, Gil?"

"So good to see you."

"You look great."

"What brings you to God's country?"

"I was hoping I'd see you again."

And so it went with each beauty falling all over herself to outpraise the other.

I was beginning to get an uncomfortable feeling.

Then Kay somehow materialized over my right shoulder and whispered into my ear, "Flirt with them all you want, but tonight you're *mine.*"

When I turned to look her in the eye, she was gone back to her other guests.

Was this what it was like for Captain Quincy? I

wondered. And if so, was it too far-fetched to think the whole crew could have boiled over with jealousy and tossed him overboard? Maybe he was strong, but five girls could handle that, especially with the aid of some sleeping pills.

That made me think. Could *I* please all of them while making each think she was the only one? What if I didn't succeed? Would they take out their anger in some permanent way? Les was a chauvinist, Les was a rounder, a bounder and a bore. Les was aggravating. Perhaps the empowerment of women had caught up with him.

But how did that square with the angry Admiral and this doyenne with a cane who gave no indication she felt much grief at her son's demise; who got the insurance payoff from the sunken boat; who exhibited as much charm to me as a kamikaze closing in on a battleship.

Ada Hatborough—the Hawaiian Tyrannosaurus Rex.

Then I looked back at the circle of beauties around me.

I had the strange feeling the girls were all dressed as they had for their interview with Les Quincy, back before he became so disastrously acquainted with Davy Jones and an anonymous shark.

Sooshe was in tight, sawed-off jeans and an un-undergirded tank top. Prudence in a sarong that clung to her for dear life—bluish with a wild print of tropical fruits. Ruth was in a black dress, not too daring, but not that modest either. Elizabeth wore a miniskirt and a miniblouse made of a material in the cellophane family.

Over at the edge of the gathering, I'd seen Ada

Hatborough, the doyenne, in a confidential huddle with the grumpy Admiral, whose eyes darted over the crowd as the doyenne was haranguing him. He was keeping tabs on his flirtatious significant other, Kay. He seemed afraid she would disappear into a bedroom with any pair of pants she could.

Felicity was near them, serving her crab cakes. Then she offered the Admiral and the doyenne her tray. The Admiral waved her off, but Ada Hatborough took one, popped it into her mouth, then took another. Felicity stepped away from them but stayed close as Ada resumed her harangue and the admiral answered her.

In a moment, I caught Felicity's eye. "Excuse me a moment, ladies," I said, "I see some food."

"Oh, let me get it," Prudence said.

"Hurry back," Ruth said

"We'll miss you," Sooshe said.

"Don't go," Elizabeth said.

When I got to Felicity, some older gentleman was bending her ear while waving one of the crab cakes on a toothpick. Felicity was listening politely, though it seemed forever, she turned from him finally to offer me her wares.

Carefully, slowly, I speared a crab cake, then changed my mind and went for another as she whispered, "She—the fat one—said, 'Those stupid bimbos are going to give the game up.' He said, 'Well, they apparently haven't so far.' She said, 'They know they're accomplices, don't they? Why do you think they're here?' Then she said, 'I say we get rid of him—'"

I didn't have to ask who "him" was.

"Then he said, 'It's all arranged.'"

Nothing would give me more pleasure than to say that news of my impending demise rolled off me like water off a chicken's back. The truth was somewhere mired in the dens of terror. The trick was in not letting it show, but at the same time keeping my back to the wall. A Russian proverb comes to mind:

Pray to God
but keep rowing
to the shore

A rigid upper lip was in order. I worked it so hard my upper lip felt like it had a charley horse.

There was a slick, shiny dance floor set up in the yard in front of the band in the Admiral's lush backyard. Everything seemed lush in Honolulu, not only the tourists. The girls competed with each other to dance with me.

Ruth got me first. I wasn't that keen on dancing, but it was an opportunity to get the girls of the crew alone to try out my theories.

After the first few bars of the music "Some Enchanted Evening" from *South Pacific,* and the first twirl, I said, "So, Ruth, I have a couple of theories—stop me if I'm wrong. Not very much you told me was true."

She looked hurt. "Why do you think that?"

"I think the only one loaded with sleeping pills that last night was the captain himself. I know the bit about everyone sleeping so soundly through it, and it worked with the police. I can't say it didn't work with me—for a while. This was just too important for any of you to sleep through."

"Why are you telling me this?"

"Because, if anyone could break with the group it would be you. You were the outsider, the oddball—"

"Thanks."

"Pleasure," I said as though I didn't grasp the insult she felt. "I think you were further out than you said and you just cut him up a bit and dumped him overboard. Probably didn't care if he died or not, just wanted to scare him to death. It was the middle of the night and he was drugged and so far from the islands, no one could swim that far."

She smiled. "It's a nice theory, but it's not right."

"I don't think you were intimate with Les either. You didn't like him. The story doesn't clean up."

"Wash," she said. "That cliché is, the story doesn't wash."

"Well, does it?"

The corner of her mouth tightened as though a smile were forthcoming. It wasn't. "I guess if you expected some outpouring of incrimination from me you are in for a disappointment."

"So, why are you all here? You weren't so lovey-dovey with each other on the ship. Just dying to see each other?"

"What do you think?" she asked.

"I think you were all in on it, you all got your stories straight and the cops bought it. Laziness? Intimidation? Just not worth the trouble, whatever. You got off easy. But Les's widow didn't buy it. You got nervous when I came snooping around. You called each other and agreed to meet here—not a bad spot to meet, I'll agree. Shore up your stories in case I sliced the case."

She giggled.

"What's so funny?"

"Nobody ever thought *you*'d crack the case."

"So, why did you seduce me?"

"I *liked* you, Gil. I like unthreatening men. There's something about you. Call it a charming magnetic vulnerability."

"Did Les have it?"

"Phew—*no!* Anything but."

"I rest my case."

The music stopped and rested my case for good. Ruth squeezed my hand. "Don't give up," she whispered.

What did she mean? She wanted me to find the truth, but she didn't want to be the one to give it to me?

Sooshe was next. "The Impossible Dream" was coming out of the band. In my arms, Sooshe seemed as light as goose down.

"So, Sooshe, why am I getting all this attention?"

"You're irresistible. We're lonely women without men." she shrugged. "Why not?"

"Isn't to cover your pretty *derrières*? Mislead me—put me off the perfume as they say."

She tittered. "Off the scent, Gil—"

"That's it?"

"That's the phrase, that's not what happened."

"So, what *did* happen?"

"I don't know—he disappeared."

"And butterflies give buttermilk. Somehow I can't swallow you are all here because you couldn't bear to be apart."

"Well—" she said. "You aren't so stupid, are you? Sure we got scared with you coming around to all of us. We didn't know what to think. You shouldn't think because we got paranoid, we're guilty of anything."

"Well, you must *think* you are guilty of *something* or you wouldn't have schlepped across the Pacific for this tearless reunion."

She got a faraway look across my shoulder as the trumpet took over the melody of "The Impossible Dream". "We were caught," she said. "The situation was impossible. It wasn't our doing."

"But you were accomplices?"

"We were...stupid," she said. "It was one side or the other. We all would have been in the drink. So we chose to stay high and dry."

I continued to pump for info—but she shook her head. "I've told you too much already." We finished the dance in silence, her head on my shoulder.

Prudence elbowed out Elizabeth for the next dance. I saw Kay with wary eyes on us. The band obliged with "The Chattanooga Choo-choo."

Pardon me boys, is that the
Chattanooga choo-choo…

"Isn't Chattanooga in Tennessee?" I asked, as we joined in the dancing pose.

"Sho is, honey chile," she said.

"Tell me, your father isn't with you, is he?"

She laughed. "No, I'm a big girl now."

"Might not be too happy to see us dancing like this."

"Might not," she said. "His problem."

"Remember those bozos that came after me when we were down by the river?"

"I remember."

"Was that your father's doing or yours?"

"Oh, maybe a little of both. We wanted to scare you but we didn't really know how."

"Why scare me?"

"Obviously we weren't eager to be sucked back into this thing."

"Back?"

"Yes, *back*. We were babes in the woods. We didn't like Les, but it wasn't so bad we'd want to kill him. The trip was over—we were going to be free of that monster."

"So, what happened?"

"Somebody obviously had other plans."

"Who?"

"Ah, that would be telling."

"So tell."

"No can do."

"Why not?"

"Because, obviously, I don't want to join Les under the sea."

"But I don't understand what you all have to fear if you didn't participate."

"Ah, yes, fear. Who does understand it? Is it always rational? Is it *ever*? Take my word for it, we're scared. See that fat Buddha over there with the Jesus necklace on? She looks like if she tried to get up, that cross would pull her back down."

"I see her."

"Don't mess with her."

"She's Les's mother."

"Yeah, was. Les is no more."

"She doesn't seem too broken up."

"They weren't the best of friends."

"Why not?"

"Les killed her husband."

"His father?"

"No. Stepfather."

"Why?"

"Couldn't stand him."

"And he wasn't even arrested?"

She shook her head. "Couldn't get anything on him."

"So, she arranged with you all to take her own son out of the picture?"

"Wouldn't put it past her," she said as though she didn't know what happened.

"So, what did happen?"

"Wish I knew," she said blithely.

"Yeah, all you know is you are completely innocent."

"Right."

"That's why you all are paying me so much attention, plying me with more lies."

"I don't think anyone's lying to you, Gil. Misleading perhaps," she said with a pixie twinkle in her eye. "Ask Kay," she said.

If anyone could mislead with greater aplomb than Prudence, it was Elizabeth.

The music for the dance with the source of the bomb in my car was "I Get a Kick Out of You—"

I get no kick from cocaine...

"I'm surprised you're dancing with me," I said. "Should I be wearing a bulletproof vest?"

"That wasn't my doing," she said.

Funny how they were all so innocent of everything.

"Whose was it?"

"Those bums who got me into that trouble in the first place."

"The drug runners?"

"I had no idea what they were doing. You trust your friends and what happens?"

"They blow up my car—expecting me to be in it?"

"Yeah," she said shaking her head as though the whole thing was beyond her comprehension.

"Only the orders for that came from the doyenne over there on the chair," I said. "Mrs. Heavyweight with the crucifix around her neck."

Elizabeth was an accomplished dancer, and she saw to it I could feel the ins and outs of her body as we moved over the shiny, slick floor.

"Oh?" Elizabeth said.

"Yeah. I expect by then things were getting a little hot in Honolulu. It was starting to bug her. The fear was one of you had weakened and I'd better be taken care of. Lucky you had those boys in tow. Those charmers who knew something about bombing cars."

"Not enough, apparently," she said, matter-of-factly.

"And while we're on the subject, why, may I ask, did you make that false statement about me in jail?"

"What are you talking about? I didn't make *any* statements in jail. Those jerks were the cause of my trouble—I knew nothing about what you were up to. That's why they left me out."

"You didn't sign any statement falsely implicating me?"

"I didn't sign anything," she said with *beaucoup* conviction.

The girls had fed me such a sugary diet I didn't know what to believe.

"One thing I can't block out, Elizabeth, is that bomb in my car. Is there any doubt the intent of that little event, or what would have happened had I not stopped for lunch?"

"That wasn't me," she said. "I don't know anything about bombs."

"No? My car in front of your house? I've just been thrown in jail because I visited you at the wrong time. Am I right in assuming those bozos were locked up when that bomb was planted?"

"Don't know, Gil, only know *I* didn't plant it."

"Butterflies," I said.

"What?"

"Butterflies are back in the dairy business."

She didn't seem to know what I meant. "Okay, Elizabeth," I said. "I'll take one more shot at it. You don't have to commit—only tell me if I'm wrong. Word spread I was getting to you all. You were last. Whoever was running this thing wanted me out of the way. My money is on Big Ada. She almost killed me herself. But I expect whoever was behind this has you scared, so I won't press. So she—or he—had that bomb planted at your place. It was prearranged. I expect your cohorts did it, but whoever did it knew it was my car and when it would be there. And *that* info had to come from *you*." I looked her in the eye. "Rebuttal?" I asked. There was none. I couldn't read the tiny smile that curled one corner of her lips.

The music ended and I put Elizabeth down as the least likely of the crowd to come forward with anything helpful. Perhaps because she had the most at stake.

I felt the presence of Kay before I saw her behind me.

"Get them out of your system," she said. "You're mine now."

All this attention was enormously flattering. Kay's invitation to see her bedroom was no exception.

The next thing I knew I was being guided by my elbow down into the house, past the open wall and a barrage of food on the tables, down a long hall reminiscent of one of those airport tunnels that was leading you to your doom.

All the girls were beautiful in their way, but tonight, on her home field, Kay was knock-down-dead gorgeous. Her blue eyes were laser and loving at the same time, her tall, lithe body hit you right in the solar plexus. Her shining blond hair was just there, framing the delicate, but savvy face like gold-leaf gilt.

En route to this anticipated ecstasy, I overheard Prudence say, "Oh God, Kay's got him. She's the reason we're in this mess in the first place."

"Hon," someone said. "If I know Kay, she'll get us out of it." I pictured Ruth, but it could have been Sooshe.

"In here, Gil," Kay purred as she opened the door and stepped inside. "I want you to see my playpen."

It didn't take much to draw me inside. Her bedroom was a force of nature, like the eye of a tornado. After I stepped inside, she reached over to lock the door. "Just a precaution," she smiled. Suddenly I felt a strange mixture and adventure and excitement commingled with a touch of fear—like an animal who'd just heard the trap door snap shut on a banquet of bait. Eat first, deal with escape later.

Kay's *boudoir* was heavy on the pinks. There were frills everywhere, lace curtains and fringy bedding.

Mosquito netting surrounded the bed like a stage curtain, rising and falling on the performance.

She looked deep into my eyes. "You have the most gorgeous eyes," she said. Then she extended her forefinger and ran it up and down the buttons on my shirt. "So, how do you like my party so far?"

"I like it," I said.

"I notice you seem taken with the help."

"Oh?" I feigned surprise, but not too convincingly.

"Oh, Gil," she said. "It's all right. We want you to like the cuties we hired to pass the hors d'oeuvres."

"Yes, I..."

"They're pretty nice, huh? Know why we do it? Dress 'em like that?"

"Well..."

"To get the blood boiling in you old parties. Then we close in for the kill and reap the benefits...something like I am doing now."

If I realized at the time my daughter, Felicity, was one of those "cuties" hired to get the old folks' blood boiling, I repressed it. All I remember is my mouth feeling like it was stuffed with polyester—or one of those fabrics.

As Kay unbuttoned my shirt I dreamily watched her tapered, tanned fingers deftly slip the buttons out of their moorings.

Felicity who?

When I looked at Kay from this intimate vantage point, it was impossible to understand her philosophy. Nobody could be more adroit at boiling blood than she was. In the debate over God being angry, jealous, vengeful, or loving, it would have to be admitted that with people like Kay peopling the earth, He had a keen eye for sensuality.

Kay did a slight, deft dance step that had me with my calves touching the edge of her bed and a kitten touching me, up and down, around and around.

And then I was down for the count—flat on my back as though I had been knocked out, and in a manner of speaking, I had been.

I was helpless to resist both mentally and physically, and Kay soon showed me resistance to her ministrations was not an option.

"Kay," I said, midstream, "why?"

"Why?" she echoed confused.

"Yeah. Why was it necessary to kill Les?"

"Oh, pooh," she said, or something like it. "Why do you want to talk about Les at a time like this?"

"Well, you *were* going to marry him, after all."

"Hmm. I told them they had nothing to fear from you—you were a lamb."

"Thanks."

"Yeah, nothing wrong with lambs."

Not known for their incisive intelligence or wit, I thought, but kept to myself.

Then before I knew it, Kay was back to the nuzzling and groping business. It seemed so effortless. It was for me.

"You're very nice," I whispered...

"Hmm, thanks—you too."

"To invite me here—and to have the whole crew," I explained.

"Oh, that," she said. "It's nothing. I feel sorry for Edna Quincy. If I can help you solve the case for her, so much the better." (We were milking the butterflies again.)

She gave me such a powerful kiss, it took the wind out of me. She knew how to make a guy forget his fear.

In the afterglow, I tried to understand Kay. Was she really interested in me? I had to doubt. Did she think the oldest lure in the books would alleviate her of complicity in the murder? Also doubtful. But I was, I thought, handed an opportunity too good to pass up.

"So, what really happened, Kay—out there on the boat—the last night?"

She looked at me with a strange twist of her lips and said, "Why would I tell you?"

I answered the look. "Because we're rather close."

She seemed to shudder at the thought of baring her bare soul, then dissolved her resolve, relieved to unburden herself.

"He had his good points, I suppose—Les," she said, as though I might not know who she was talking about. "But he wasn't really a very nice person..."

"So, you popped him overboard?"

"Not that simple," she said.

"Nothing is," I said.

"They made me do it. His mother, the Admiral, but if you ever tell, I'll deny it. There is *no* evidence."

"As long as you can keep four young women from spouting off. Can you?"

"Listen, we had nothing to do with what happened to him. I just gave Les sleeping pills to make it easier for him. It was going to happen anyway, so what I did was humanitarian."

"Did you give pills to the other girls?"

She shook her head.

"Was he alive or dead when they threw him overboard?"

"Alive. That was the plan. We could always fall back on that if the worst came. Nobody wanted to kill him, just scare him."

"So, you didn't cut him up to attract sharks?"

"No."

"The plan?"

"Les was getting uppity and no one liked that. He was a child, really, and had to be dealt with as a child, or so Ada thought. Ada was this big Christian. Les rebelled. He did everything she loathed. Sometimes I thought all his debauching was just to get his mother's goat. He just *hated* her second husband.

"When Ada heard Les was taking a Christian on board to do his little thing to her, Ada decided her boy needed a little religion himself. So she had this idea to scare the bejesus out of him. To say nothing of the trick he pulled on his mother's second husband."

"What trick?"

"He killed her second husband."

"He did? How? Why?"

"They hated each other. The stepson, the stepfather. Hamlet. Lot of baggage in those relationships."

"How did he do it?"

"Stanley had a heart condition. Needed nitroglycerin pills to stay alive. He'd have these attacks and he'd have to pop a pill on the spot. He had an attack when Ada was gone and Les was in the house. Les didn't give him the pills. Let him die."

"Why didn't they go to the police?"

"Because it's not a crime, technically. Killing with pills is murder. Withholding life-saving pills is nothing."

"So in retribution, Ada had her son killed? A mother would *do* that?"

Kay shook her head. She was trailing her fingers lazily on my bare chest. "Not so simple," she said. "Despite his macho swagger, Les was really a little boy. He was dependent on his mother. Oh, he was married and all, but he was a momma's boy to the end. It was a love/hate thing. She bought the boat. But there was this Hamlet thing. Stanley—her second hubby—was *very* sensual. Les couldn't take it."

"Weird," I said. "So how did the pill thing work with Stanley?"

"Ada was away on one of her Christian things, and Les just hid Stanley's pills. I wasn't there of course, but I can just imaging Les riling Stanley up until he *needed* those pills to live. Then he doesn't give them. Stanley can't move and he finally dies. Les leaves the house so Ada finds Stanley when she comes home. Only she finds the pills hidden in the dishwasher and she knows...

"She shifts her retaliation gear into high. Cuts

off his funds, but Les has a wife with some money in New Mexico. Now, Les may be a hopeless juvenile delinquent, but nobody could say "No" to him, and his wife financed the last cruise. Ada was fit to be tied. Then of course he got this second generation hippie preggers and that didn't sit too well with the *grande dame*, either. Ada was well on edge with it all but I think his hiring Ruth for the crew, and in keeping with his charming nature, flaunting it to his mother—it was just the last straw."

"The camel needed a chiropractor."

"What? Oh, I get it—the camel's back was broken—No, Gil, I'd say the camel needed an orthopedic surgeon, but anyway, Ruth was okay and all, but she didn't in any way fit Les's blueprint for a crew member." Kay stopped to titter. "And, by God he had his way with her. Couldn't *wait* to tell his mother. We sailed close enough in so his cell phone worked and he just rubbed Ada's nose in it. I think then she *wanted* to kill him—mother or no—"

"So you did?"

"No, no. Why would we do that?"

"Because you all hated him, too—"

"Well, that's not strictly true. He was annoying, could be maddening, but he was also so blessedly sexy. A little boy, yes, but a macho stud on top of it, too."

"So, don't tell me, he just fell overboard?"

"Not exactly. It started as a lark," she said, frowning. "Almost a joke. We were going to drug him with sleeping pills, then tie him over the side and all be standing over him when he came to."

"Didn't work?"

"He was a heavy sucker. It took all of us to

move him up on deck. He came to, sort of, enough to make it harder to get him over the side. We'd tied him up, of course, but in the process of pushing him over, his rump hit a jagged screw on a winch or something and he bled some. By the time we got him in the water and tied to the anchor hoist, there was enough blood in the water to attract sharks."

"But like the trick with his stepfather, you didn't save him?"

"We tried. We had only the briefest of moments of glory when he came to enough to realize what was happening. And he looked up at five pair of gloating eyes and we saw the pleading in his eyes and then suddenly terror as one of the sharks took the first piece of him."

"Or her first piece..."

"What? Oh, the shark a female? Sure, poetic justice. Well, we panicked. It didn't take us long to realize what it looked like—it looked like murder. We pulled him up out of the water, but by the time we were able to get him above the water line—it was a real battle with the sharks, and well, we lost the battle. Anyway, when we finally got him up there, we saw his legs were gone and he was unconscious. The other girls screamed. I was too scared to. There may have been a brief discussion about more blood on the boat incriminating us beyond our intention, and we couldn't save him, anyway."

"So you let him sink back into the drink unceremoniously. Gone but not forgotten. The best laid plans of rodents and men..."

Kay stopped her caressing. "What would *you* have done, Gil?" she asked with forlorn eyes that could have drawn birds from the rose bushes.

"I don't know why you couldn't tell that to the police." But even as I said it, I knew why. Manslaughter for all of them, involuntary manslaughter if they were lucky. Acquittal possible, but not worth the chance. Instead, they stuck to a simple story. Monkey see no evil, hear no evil, speak no evil.

"We did the best we could cleaning up the blood, but when she saw it, Ada didn't think it was good enough. So—goodbye boat."

The only question left to me was why would she tell me all this? Certainly it compromised her and her friends.

Then I had my answer: I heard a key turning in Kay's locked bedroom door.

I heard a door opening and felt Kay throw the satin sheet over me at the same time.

Funny how I knew the act was fruitless and wouldn't fool a blind man and yet offered me a strange, short-lived comfort. As though the darkness would shut out the danger.

I heard Kay say angrily, "The door was locked, Admiral." No honey or anything. She called him Admiral. Admirable.

"You slut!" he said, as though he had met the enemy at last. Seemed a strange appellation after all that business on the boat with Les and the girls, but passions run deep in these waters.

I felt him beside me at the bed. Then the covers were yanked back and I did the best to hide my blushing nakedness as though that would allow me to die modestly. For I was looking down the barrel of a cannon from one of the Admiral's battleships. Perhaps I exaggerate a tad, but from my vantage point that's what it looked like.

The Admiral suddenly looked taller, more macho, more powerful, more relaxed. Naturally, he was, as they say, packing the heat. I expected to feel it, briefly, at any moment.

"I told you, you were *persona non grata* around here, but you never got the word. Some recruits *never* get the word." He clucked his tongue at the overburdening sadness.

"I..." I began a weak, mindless protest.

"You insisted on poking your nose into the merciful death of that no-good murderer who took my best friend's life as sure as he had shot him between the eyes..." Then he added as a cheery afterthought, "like I am going to do to you."

He didn't make mincemeat of words. The Admiral was a man of action. I knew it was anchors aweigh time.

He squeezed the trigger.

The cold terror of facing the business end of a gun with a grumpy military man with a grudge behind it is not a moment you'd ever forget, should you live through it.

The explosion came from the Admiral not his gun, when he shouted "Damn!"

The gun hadn't fired. It took the Admiral only a moment before he shot his accusation—"You emptied my gun!" It was an admission of emasculation from the Admiral.

"Honey," she said. "Killing him wasn't such a good idea."

"He's vermin!"

"No, he's a cuddly teddy bear," she said, and reached out in her nudity to embrace me. Even in my stress I could appreciate the art of her body. But not for long. The Admiral threw the gun at us and it hit me square on the arm. It smarted.

"You ruined it." he exclaimed at Kay. "Made me look like a fool."

"Oh, honey," she said. "Gil and I'll get dressed

and we can talk about the agreement."

I didn't know what she was talking about, but I was not in any condition to argue. "If we can't get Gil to agree, then you can shoot him."

I gagged at that one. How insignificant I must have been to her after all that teddy-bear talk.

We got dressed and I became aware of the party outside for the first time since I entered Kay's intimate sanctum. I pictured the other four beauties out there enjoying themselves, not exactly wallowing in their guilt, as Ada Hatborough lunged into the room, the heavy crucifix around her neck propelling her forward. She shot bullets of her own glare through me and waved her cane inches from my nose—so close I looked at the floor to see if she had gotten it. She took possession of one of the chairs in the room as though she were testing it for strength prior to repossessing it. Kay sat on the edge of the bed and I sat on a chair beside it, both of us facing the great, august Admiral who was beginning to put me in mind of the great Elbert August Wemple, that realtor ass I worked for.

The Admiral stood over us.

The Admiral began as though addressing a ship full of sailors.

He stared at Kay a moment before cocking a crooked eye at me. "She told you the story, I presume?"

"She told me *a* story," I said. "I have no corroboration."

He nodded and looked back at Kay as if to say, "I knew it." Without taking his eyes from his significant co-host, he said, "Bet she didn't tell you the truth."

Now I looked at Kay. Was she blushing or was

she flushed with anger?

"Oh, Admiral," she said, shortly. "Why do you want to rehash all that? It has nothing to do with anything."

I was hoping he'd rehash away, but I wasn't optimistic. I was wrong.

"I suppose Kay told you this business with Les was all Ada's idea."

"Well..." I looked at Kay who was looking away.

The Admiral held out a hand to forestall any further effort on my part. "Oh, I know Kay—she told you it was Ada who wanted to scare him, didn't she? Teach him a lesson. Give him religion, even. It was always a disappointment for a woman of deep faith to have such a debauching son."

I decided against answering, since he plowed on anyway. "Told you, I expect, she came to Honolulu to find her biological father—"

"Yes, I..."

"Tell you who he was?"

"Mentioned a name maybe, but...wait a minute!" Then it hit me like a kilo of bricks: Stanley was—Stanley. The Stanley Kay told me about. "Kay's father and Les's *step*father," I said as though I had just discovered the Dominican Republic.

"Yes, exactly. Ada's second husband and," he paused to pay obeisance to an inner emotion and exchange glances with Ada, "my best friend."

"So it was Kay's idea to..."

"Exactly!" he said.

I had a feeling he was not as broadminded about being cuckolded—in a manner of speaking—as I was led to believe. "Ada was devastated, I was devastated, but Kay took it the hardest of all. She had the inside track on getting on the crew. Les didn't know her, but she knew Ada. This whole scheme was her own little idea. Told everyone Les was going to marry her. Hah! Les wouldn't have married the most desirable woman in the world. He was far too selfish for that."

Kay got a twinkle in her moist eyes. "But honey, don't you think I am the most desirable woman in the world?"

"Sometimes," he snorted.

I looked over to where Kay was seated on the edge of the bed— "You *did* want to kill him," I said.

She shook her head and fought back the tears. "I went on board thinking I could kill him, but the longer I was on—" she broke down, pulled a Kleenex from the night stand at the side of the bed, blew her nose and thus fortified, shook her head again as if to clear it of ugly memories. "I don't know what happened. I... I actually did fall in love with him—in spite of myself. Maybe it was the scent of the competition. The challenge of making him like me best."

"Did you succeed?" I asked.

She didn't answer right away. "For awhile," she said. "But Les...he tired of women. That's why he took five, I guess. But Les...he could have used ten or twenty in those three months."

"So you got angry."

"Of course I did," she snapped. "We *all* got mad as hell at him."

"So you killed him?"

Slowly, she shook her head, as though she weren't sure. "No," she said at last, "but we did want to scare the hell out of him. I did, anyway. I don't want to blame the others. But no one tried to stop me, and...with what happened, they all knew...well, let's just say they all knew how it would look to anyone."

"And that's the truth?" I asked, and looked at the Admiral for verification. He tightened his lips.

Kay nodded. "The sharks got him—it was that cut, I guess. I didn't know about sharks."

"Then you blew up the boat so there would be no trace?"

"That was Ada's idea. She wanted closure. She wanted the insurance, not the boat."

I saw Ada clutch her cane and lurch forward. The Admiral held up a hand and she sank back.

"You know, Mr. Yates, murdering someone with pills is a crime. Murdering someone by withholding pills is not a crime. The crime is in the act, you see. But can you honestly say deliberately keeping a dying man from the medicine that will save his life is not murder?"

"I don't make laws," I said. "I don't even enforce them."

Ada didn't like that—she muttered "Smartmouth," and started to rise, but gravity was against her. The Admiral didn't like it either.

"Do you realize, young man, that he murdered my friend just as sure as if he'd pulled the trigger? Why? He didn't like him. That's all. That's the kind of scum he was. He took everything he wanted and if he didn't like you, why you didn't deserve to live! Is this a man we should mourn?"

"I'm not a judge," I tried again.

"So, this will just be our secret?" Kay asked.

"Well, I've been hired to look into this case. If I don't tell my principal what I learned, I don't earn my fee."

A playful smile crossed Kay's lips—a feeling of relaxing of tension seemed to spread throughout her body. "We'll double it," she said with a confidence obviously born of mistaken assumptions.

My turn for the fun. "Oh," I said with a raised eyebrow, "I don't think you will."

"Try me," she taunted.

"Obviously you think I work like the…" here I paused for, I will admit, a self-satisfied effect, "…run-of-the-mill detective."

"A thousand a day and expenses? Is it *that* much, Mr. Yates?"

For whose benefit was she calling me Mr. Yates? I wondered. Looking at her I decided it was all she could to keep from tittering.

"What do you have—fifteen to twenty days, Mr. Yates?"

"Actually, I don't charge by the day," I said, trying to under bravado the thing. "I charge on a contingency basis—a prearranged fee payable only if I succeed."

"Well, you succeeded, and now you have a chance to double your fee." The Admiral was putting his four cents in. "How much was it, Mr. Yates?"

"I don't know if I am at liberty to discuss my fee without my client's approval."

"Well then, call her up," he said. "It's four hours later there."

I knew I was going to tell them my fee. I wasn't going to add anything about the easy payment plan Edna Quincy and I had agreed on. But I was having so much fun building to the optimum effect, I held out a tad too long.

"Oh, why should we mess with such a small-timer," the Admiral said in disgust, as though I were a mere barnacle on a battleship. "He's probably getting five or ten grand and he wants to make that look important."

"Two hundred thousand," I said with a cocky air that was completely foreign to Malvin Stark, but was becoming part and package of the Gil Yates persona.

There was a stunned silence in the group. Then a sputtering from one head, then another.

The doyenne broke the silence. "Edna Quincy doesn't *have* that kind of money," she said, with a confident outthrust of her chest, but I could see a slight doubt that she knew everything.

I rolled my eyes in that that's-what-you-think fashion.

"Well, I..." she was chewing on the possibility and it was distasteful to her. "Very well, then," she said, with a stentorian thrust of her ample jaw. "We'll double that."

There it was, the age-old temptation, honor or cash? I wasn't naïve enough to think the extra two hundred grand would wean me from Elbert A. Wemple Realtor Ass., but it would put some mighty nice cycads in my backyard.

I started to shake my head when I saw the liver-spotted hand of the Admiral rise up to staunch the heresy. "Before you reject it out of hand, I want to make sure you grasp the import of the matter to us. I think I speak for all of us when I say we are none of us willing to take the harassment of criminal charges—though I don't doubt we could defeat them."

He doubted it.

"Without making a threat, I think it might be wise of you to realize the fate that befell Les Quincy could befall...any of us."

"Really?" I said, looking from one expectant face to another. "Any of...us... could be thrown to the sharks?"

The Admiral tightened his lips and nodded his head with a curt, military snap.

"So, when you say any of us, you are including the women?" I asked, looking at the not-so-innocent faces of Ada and Kay.

Another military snap of the head.

I shook my head with as much sadness as I could fake. It wasn't *sadness* I felt, but cold fear.

"So, then," I mushed on, "anyone could include you and Kay?"

The head didn't snap anymore. I thought the top would blow off like the Mauna Loa volcano. His face reddened and I didn't have to guess he was at the end of his chain of command.

"That's it!" he blew like Moby Dick. He threw his arm out at me and grabbed my pitiful biceps with such force that I was forced to consider my best interests.

Before I had time to think, the formidable Ada Hatborough had risen to the occasion—no small feat for one of her imposing stature—and advanced on me with her cane drawn as a weapon. Just before she came within caning distance she began flailing the air with the silver machete—or so it seemed to me, and it was only a matter of seconds before I considered looking to the floor for my head.

"Okay," I cringed, and held up my arms to

block the impending blows. "Let's work out the details," I gasped. "God is love," I said, I don't know why. The cane sliced the air once again in my direction.

After that excitement, things settled down. I was a little sorry it was so easy (very little). I walked out of there with a check made out to Gil Yates for four-hundred thousand dollars.

Of course, the Admiral wasn't born just a few days ago. He thought it best for all concerned if we signed a friendly agreement that stated the consideration was a kind donation from concerned friends because I had spent so much time on the case without coming to any conclusions, and since I had worked on a contingency basis and would lose that, they were compensating me for my diligent efforts, and of course, in the unlikely event that I was compensated by someone else, I would forfeit their "donation."

I don't want to sound like I was a sellout, but I thought it was the prudent thing to do to get out of there alive. I could work out the details later. I hadn't committed to taking the check, only to not spilling the corn if I cashed it. I had quickly planned to dart through of the house without returning to the backyard party and the rest of the crew. I was uncomfortable facing them now that I knew their secrets.

But they were waiting at the door when I came out of the bedroom and I felt like I was covered from head to toe with lipstick and good wishes that may have lacked a certain sincerity. I waved at Felicity who stunned me by waving back. There was even a smile with it. There may be hope for the kid yet.

When I was finally clear of that den of iniquity, it hit me—I had an ethical dilemma: my client's interests or my own.

Decisions like that, I've found, are best put off to another day. I would wait until after the plane trip home. Chances are the thing would crash and I wouldn't have to make the decision. Of course, I could call Edna Quincy from Honolulu and let the dog out of the bag, but for some reason, I wanted to be home first. The high risk of airplane travel notwithstanding, I thought my chances of staying alive were better if I got out of Honolulu as soon as possible.

All in all I was pleased that I was leaving Honolulu with a check for four hundred grand in my chest pocket rather than with a bullet in my chest. The parting reminded me we were all birds made out of the same feathers. Pals, buddies, co-conspirators.

On the flight home the stewardess (p.c. flight attendant) flopped down some canned orange juice and an aluminum sack with a thimble full of peanuts on my tray. She was Methuselah's cousin, and it was the high spot of the trip.

The guy next to me talked nonstop, and it didn't seem to bother him that I wasn't listening. The gist of what he said seemed to be he was one cool cat and nobody could handle women the way he could.

A look at him offered several possibilities:

1. There was no accounting for taste.
2. He was deluded, big time.
3. We hadn't seen the women.

When I got home, Tyranny Rex was out as she

usually was. How does that cute expression go? Out like a light? Tyranny rather was out like the dark. Out of sight; I don't mind.

I headed right for my palms and cycads. It had been cold for Southern California and whenever the Fahrenheit flirts with freezing one has to be solicitous of his palms. Or her palms, I suppose, though palm collecting seems to be a guy thing. Women seem more smitten with flowers, while the miracle of procreation as evidenced by palm seeds, cycad pollen and reproduction seem more fascinating to men.

Four hundred thousand dollars all at once, or two hundred thousand piecemeal? That was the question. Whether it is nobler in the minds of men to sell out for top dollar or to take half while striving for ethical purity, *that* is the question.

I looked at the space between palms and speculated what cycads would fit nicely there, considering exposure to sun, protection from wind, eventual crowding (when I was a hundred years old). Four hundred grand would make the skids a lot greasier.

What did I owe Edna Quincy anyway? I gave it a shot. I don't produce, she doesn't pay.

And I had become rather fond of the young ladies who sailed that shapely ship or sailed the ship shapely as the case may be. I was not a man to fake intimacy lightly. To turn my back on a paramour. What were financial considerations next to that?

My *Encephalartos paucidentatus* was getting three new leaves. A banner day for a paucie. So was the *Encephalartos woodii x natalensis.* I don't have a *woodii.* They are extinct in the wild and sell in the five-thousand-dollar range for a fairly small, young plant. They are hard to find, but with four hundred grand I could find one.

Okay, it was time to call Edna Quincy with my report. I could go to the office of Elbert A. Wemple Realtor Ass., but I thought it would be prudent to get the case closed before I subjected myself to that colossal windbag. It would only push me to the larger check.

After a lifetime of subjugation to the Wemples, a lifetime under the penurious thumb of a man whose joints were so tightly aligned he was able to produce squeaking sounds at the same time he ambulated, it was pure pleasure to have to make decisions in the hundreds of thousands.

I sat at the phone in the kitchen and dialed Edna Quincy's number. There was a scissors on the counter. While the phone rang I cut out of the four-hundred thousand dollar check a silhouette of a shapely woman. The four-hundred thousand dollars that was written on the check coincided with her upper anatomy—emblazoned across her prominent mammary glands.

By the time Edna and I finished talking, I had cut out four more of them. They seemed so flimsy and insignificant in the paper version.

Excerpts from *Bluebeard's Last Stand*
A Gil Yates Private Investigator Novel
By Alistair Boyle

Harriet was sitting in the Oak Room where she had already obtained a vodka and tonic which was sitting in front of her on the small, low chrome-legged table topped with smoke glass. A little swizzle stick in the glass pointed up to her like a beacon of shining light at the grand opening of some used car lot. Harriet was not a car, true, but sitting there alone in this macho-decor men's saloon, she did look used.

"Well, Mr. Yates," she proclaimed in her little dictator manner, "I don't suppose you'd join me in a drink. You don't approve of drinking!" and she punctuated the statement with a pucker of her face.

I sat quickly before the invitation could be withdrawn. "Where did you get that idea?"

"You don't drink, do you?"

"No, but I don't pass judgment either," I said meekly. "So, what are you doing about the burning question of the cruise?" I asked.

She smiled as the cat who had swallowed the canned fairy. "I'm thinking," she said, adding a teasing wink.

"Thinking pro or con?"

"He's a nice man," she said, sipping her booze, "I do like being with him, and from my vantage point that's the most important thing. I know from experience I'm not always that easy to be with, so I'm lucky from that standpoint. But..." she sighed and trailed off.

I waited. She took another sip. I noticed for the first time quite a little went down the hatch with those sips.

"There are a lot of differences between us, don't you see?" It may have been my imagination, but I thought she cranked up the British inflections when she began talking of differences.

"How different?" I asked.

"*My* ancestors came over on the Mayflower," she

said, as though that explained everything. I didn't mention the well-mauled suspicion that if a tiny fraction of the claimed ancestral Mayflower passengers really rode the old tub, it either made an awful lot of trips or it would have sunk before it left the dock. I would hope that if she were to throw up this canard to Reginald he would say "My family came later, they sent their servants on the Mayflower." Lord, how many "genealogists" made a fortune tying families to the Mayflower? Often with an eight- to twelve-generation gap, but I didn't question Harriet. I didn't want her to marry him, after all.

"His folks missed the boat?" I asked her.

"In a *big* way. They came over the generation he was born to. And from *Poland*," she said, putting on that sour face again, which no one could do better.

"Poland?" I said, shocked. "Windsor is a *Polish* name?"

"Of course, not," she said, "he changed it. It was Kantor. He's *Jewish!*" she said. "My ancestors would roll over in their graves!"

"Why?"

"Well in *those* days it was *declassé* to date a Jewish man."

Date? I thought. What a happy choice of words. "Well, fortunately we're over that," I said.

"Oh, don't be too sure. A lot of my friends turn up their noses when they see the size of *his* nose. *Reginald Windsor* or no!"

"Well, it's good *you* don't feel that way."

"But that's just it. I *do* sometimes," she said. "Then there are all the terminated marriages we have had between us—fourteen in all. Do we really need to do that again?"

She went on to tell me quite candidly about all the stuff in the Pinkerton report.

"Would you like another drink?" I asked.

"Yes, I would."

The waiter came right over. He had anticipated her wish and set down before her a fresh vodka and tonic.

"I like vodka because it doesn't make your breath smell," she explained.

"Does he, I mean, he certainly doesn't admit killing any of his wives, does he?"

"Oh, no. Says they're all accidents. Makes him extra solicitous of me. Anytime I get near the edge of anything he gets nervous and pulls me back."

I thought, what a nice set up. She'll trust him and one day, instead of pulling, he'll push.

"He watches me in the bathtub every minute so I won't slip."

"That's nice."

"I think so," she said.

"So you aren't afraid if you marry him, you'll have a sudden bad accident?"

"Oh, no, not Reginald, he's a lamb. Besides, he inherited money from the others. He wouldn't from me."

"How come?"

"Harvey, my son, insists I make a prenuptial agreement so he and his sister will get their mitts on the money. I've talked it over with Reginald. He's agreeable to anything."

"He seems like a very agreeable sort," I agreed.

"He *is*," she emphasized.

"So you *are* going to marry him?"

"I'm still thinking. My son, Harvey, thinks it's foolish for a seventy-six year old, married five times, to think about it again. But all my marriages were long. Well, all but one, and another who died. I was married to Harvey's father for almost twenty years. After we divorced I had my rebound marriage, a huge mistake. He was a crazy. Lasted just under two years which seemed like ten years too long.

"Then I married the General, and he died in less than a year."

"What from?"

"An accident. He fell in the tub. He drank a lot and was getting so old. Then the doctor. We had almost nine good years before he died in a car crash."

"Drinking?"

"I am afraid so. They think he might have had a heart attack at the wheel. The car crashed into a telephone pole," she sighed at the memory. "My last husband lived four years after we married. But he was almost ninety when he died."

Now I was beginning to wonder. Did she have a hand in any of those demises?

She read my mind. "I didn't get much money from any of them. My money's from my father."

"So, do you think you'll marry Reginald?"

"Possibly," she said. "If I could only win Harvey over. Reginald says I raised that boy and he hasn't been too grateful. Likes to blame all his troubles on me."

"What are his troubles?"

"He never amounted to much on his own. He's jealous of his sister and her husband's success."

"What was Harvey's father like?" I asked.

"A lot like Harvey, actually," Harriet said. "He was always looking for the big, easy dollar. His second wife was rich, but after she died he blew it all, and now the easy money continues to elude him."

"Gee," I said. "This sounds familiar."

She nodded. "When you've lived as long as I have, you keep seeing repeats of what you've already experienced, don't you see?"

"May I ask you a personal question?" I smiled ingratiatingly.

"Ask away."

"Are you ever afraid that Reginald will, well, hurt you in some way?"

Suddenly I felt cold hands tighten around my throat.

That familiar man's voice spoke behind me. "She's not afraid, but you better be."

I felt my eyes bulging, ready to pop from my forehead like two marbles in the barrels of a double-barreled shot gun. Then little squiggly worms swam in the blackness.

Then they stopped swimming.

Excerpts from *The Unlucky Seven*
A Gil Yates Private Investigator Novel
By Alistair Boyle

"How'd the audition go?" I asked as he hustled into the narrow deli with his duffel bag slung on a shoulder. In that section of the Big Applesauce, storefronts rented by the front-foot. So you had a lot of places that were about eight-feet wide and three-miles deep. The best tables were those you could reach without falling over from heat exhaustion.

"I was pleased," he said. "Trouble is, *they* have to be pleased, so you're always on pins and needles."

We made our way to a table, a distance of what some years ago would have constituted a summer vacation.

When we sat, he put his duffel bag on the floor at his feet, and said, "I ran into Greg at the audition—I asked him to join us when he finished—I hope that's all right. I haven't seen him in ages."

I waved a hand, as though I was one blasé dude. Actually, I was a little disappointed that my son wanted a buddy along for our too-infrequent meetings.

"Oh, here's Greg"—and he seemed to light up more at the sight of Greg than he had for his own father.

Greg slid into the chair next to August. They smiled, touched, rolled their eyes and raised their eyebrows, as they relived the audition and catted about some of their competition.

The waitress dragged herself to the table, as though under some internal protest. She took out her pad and wet her finger, then applied it to flip to the appropriate page.

That was, she made clear, the sum total of the communicative effort she was willing to expend in our behalf. I ordered the pastrami with everything; August and Greg agreed to split one of those concoctions recommended by Anorexics Anonymous.

I tried to bring Greg into the conversation. Though what I was doing, was trying to bring myself into the conversation.

"What do you guys think of this conspiracy bomber?"

"The Seven guy?" Greg said. "Creepy." I'm not sure August knew who we were talking about. He never seemed too taken with murder and mayhem. "Who were the victims?—Fenster of Softex, of course. The CIA guy, and who was the other one?"

"Philip Carlisle—United Motors."

Greg shrugged, "Big, rich, powerful guys. Maybe that's a risk you have to take."

"You think so?" I said. "Random killings?"

"Aren't random," Greg said. "Anything but. Very individual—targeted."

"You think there could be something to the idea seven people ruled the world?"

"I've heard crazier stuff," Greg said.

"You?" I asked August.

"I won't go for any number of world rulers unless fearless Elbert August Wemple is among them."

I'll say this for the kid, he knew how to win my approval.

"Made a lot of enemies," Greg mumbled.

"What's that?"

"Some of those guys made a lot of enemies. Take Fenster. Stepped on a lot of bodies to get where he is. There's a guy *I* could believe ruled the world."

"Why?"

"Nobody gets in his way. And the competition along the way didn't roll over and play dead. He had to roll them over. A young kid like that isn't going to be worth eight to ten billion without ruffling a few feathers."

"Yeah, I guess."

"But it's a real tragedy. He just got married—built a huge house."

"But you aren't surprised somebody killed him?"

"No. When you are so successful and so beloved in some quarters, you are bound to engender the opposite feelings in equal magnitude."

"Do you know anything about the other victims of

this latest bomber?"

"Nah. Just Fenster."

"Nothing that would tie them up?"

"No, except that it is virtually impossible to live in the world and *not* be tied up with Bob Fenster. If having ties to him and his product was the criterion for killing, you'd have to nuke the whole country."

We finished our sandwiches, and I left Miss Congeniality a tip commensurate with her charm and grace.

I thanked Greg for his information, and asked if I might call him if I had more questions.

"I'll keep in touch with August," he said. "I move around a lot."

My son and I hugged briefly, and I thought I put a little more into it than he did.

August and Greg disappeared down the street. They seemed quite content to have put me behind them. The only thing that salved my feelings was August had not asked about his mother.

Excerpts from *The Missing Link*
A Gil Yates Private Investigator Novel
By Alistair Boyle

He certainly was fond of talking. More than I am fond of listening. And of all places to experience logorrhea, a meeting of palm nuts should rightfully be near the bottom. There is zero communication with palm trees. Oh, a lot of people talk to them, but there is no documentary proof that any of them have ever talked back.

My new buddy is a gardener for one of the super-rich. Mr. Rich's got a whale of a palm collection, so Jack Kimback is here to bone up.

Now Jack gets to the meat of the thing. His boss, who is just too famous, in an illicit sort of way, to mention, is looking for a private detective to find his daughter.

He has interviewed every known agency, tried a few, and doesn't like any of them. He is apparently a very picky man, as can be seen in his hiring this erudite, well-spoken young man to tend his palms.

Said Megabucks has also had it with the cops and the missing persons folks. A man that rich, his gardener says, is used to buying what he wants, but his money, this time, isn't cutting the ketchup.

If you have ever felt possessed by the devil, you know how I felt when I heard the following words come out of my mouth:

"Oh, I just happen to *be* a private detective."

Jack's eyebrows hit the ceiling. You could tell he was skeptical that a mealy-mouthed guy like me would be in such a macho line of work.

It seemed like a harmless tease at first. I didn't look on it as a lie, exactly. A lark. I thought it would go no further. Any time now, I would set him straight–tell him I was only joking. But the more he told me, the more intrigued I became, and the less impetus I had for telling the technical truth.

You know what the "technical truth" is. It is something that only serves the science of mathematics. Every other human endeavor is necessarily fraught with nuances, with shadings, with spared feelings, with personal aggrandizement. Call a spade a spade? Only when you are playing cards.

"I'll give him your card," Jack said, putting his hand out for a card, as though that would be an easy end to it.

"I don't have cards," I heard myself say, "that's for small-timers."

His eyebrows were on the rise again.

"Well, give me your name and office address, he'll have somebody check you out."

"I'm not a guy who sits in an office," I said, astonishing even myself with the dire depths of my deception. "Results is my middle name. And," I added with just the right touch of hauteur, "my phone is unlisted."

"So how do people get a hold of you?"

"They don't," I said. "I call them."

Now the dark eyebrows went whacko. "You don't know my boss," he said.

"And maybe I'd be just as well-off getting through life without knowing him."

He frowned and gave a curt nod that he must have thought was noncommittal.

"Tell you what," I said. "Let him know we talked. I'll call you in a couple days. If he's interested, I'll meet him." Then I added, unknowingly, the clincher: "By the way, I work like the ambulance-chasing lawyers: I don't find his daughter, I don't get paid."

A smile crossed his face, like a man realizing the razor being held at his neck was just for shaving. "He'll like that," he said, writing his phone number on a photocopy of a walking tour of the palms at Bernuli Junior College. "Sometimes he's so tight, he squeaks."

"She was anorexic," he said softly, a little ashamed. "Bulimic. I tried to help her. I couldn't do anything. I put her in an institution. The best money could buy," he hastened to add, unnecessarily. He paused to control his breathing–to drain the flush from his face. "She escaped. Hasn't been seen since."

"How long ago?"

"Nine months or so."

"Been to the police? The FBI? Missing persons?"

He stared at me as though it were a naive question. "She's an adult. They seemed to spit on me. They went through some motions," he said. "Nothing came of it." Then he added, as though it surprised him, "I think they resented me."

"Why?"

"The way they acted. What do cops make now–twenty, thirty a year? Bound to be some resentment," he said, waving his hand to encompass his expensive property. "I never felt comfortable with them."

"Do you feel comfortable with me?"

He gave me the frozen fish eye. "I don't know yet."

"What is it you want? Just a notice that she is alive–or dead–or physical possession?"

He looked at me as though his nose were a gunsight. "Well, I would expect to see her," he said. "I mean, I don't doubt your integrity, but I'd have to have the physical evidence."

"Is it possible she won't want to see you?"

Darts came through the eyes. "Why would she not?" he faltered. I think I heard his voice break. "Of course...it's...possible." He put a spin on "possible," like anything was possible but he would just as soon not think it could be in this case. When he regained his composure, he asked, "So what would you charge?"

Here we were at the moment of truth. I had rehearsed my blasé response to this inevitable question in front of the bathroom mirror in our tract house. I had honed it to as near believable perfection as I was capable of bringing off. But now my tongue seemed to stick to my lower teeth. Michael Hadaad didn't let his gaze waver. Finally I shook my head, once. "Phew," I said with as much bravado as my thumping heart would allow. "Gonna be expensive."

"How expensive?" he asked, cocking an eye of suspicion.

"Not so simple," I said. "I bring her here and she's happy to come, I'd settle for two hundred."

"Two hundred dollars?" He thought he had gotten lucky.

"Two hundred thousand," I corrected him.

"Two..." he choked. "That's ridiculous!"

This is where my art came in. I nodded, the soul of understanding, and stood to leave. I nodded again, in acknowledgment of his hospitality, and said, "I quite understand. My fees are a lot higher than the run of the mill. There are many available for a lot less."

He just stared at me, as though I were the first person to ever walk out on him. For my part, I was not as bummed at the prospect of losing the case or the fee–it was a lark anyway–as I was of losing the opportunity to see his palm collection.

I turned to leave. I had not taken three steps when I heard the mighty Michael Hadaad say, "No, wait."

I smiled to myself before I turned. Now I cocked my eye–as he had done so expertly.

He answered: "You had the guts to get up. Most people can't see past their fee. Sit down."

I did.

"Is there room for negotiation?"

"I don't nickel and dime," I said. "I don't submit chits for meals and gas. But I'm afraid I've only given you the low side."

Up went the eyelids.

I nodded. God, I thought, is he buying this? But how could he? "If she doesn't want to come, it will be a half-million."

He sank back in his chair. I stood again, but faced him. "I quite understand your reluctance, Mr. Hadaad. I am used to working for the extremely wealthy, exclusively."

He waved me back into my seat, without looking.

Excerpts from *The Con*
A Gil Yates Private Investigator Novel
By Alistair Boyle

I have always had a soft spot in my heart for a con man. I'm not sure why. He is usually a man (sorry, ladies, most of them seem to be men) who makes his living outsmarting those who are smarter than he is.

He usually plays on the greed and the get-rich-without-working nature of people who have had more education and advantages than he had. People who should know better.

So looking for the most successful and most elusive con man was an assignment I couldn't resist.

The call came from the big man himself, Franklin d'Lacy. There was no baloney with an intermediary secretary. No executive wait while the honcho cleared his throat.

"Mr. Yates," he spoke clearly, distinctly into my voice mail at the phone company, with a clipped diction that put you in mind of the British Empire. It was only an affectation, though a very good one. "Your services have been recommended to me by a member of our board, and I would appreciate a return phone call at your earliest convenience."

d'Lacy was all smiles as he rose to greet me. "So good of you to come, Yates," he beamed. I could see in a flash why he was so good at raising bucks for his museum. (He always referred to it as "my museum". It didn't win him any extra friends.)

He was the quintessential salesman, but way too suave for used cars. High-end real estate, maybe, or mainframe computers.

He struck me as a guy sensitive of his height, but he wasn't that short. At five foot, eleven-some inches I was taller, but only by a couple of inches. He was dressed in one of those banker, pin-stripe, Brooks Brothers worsteds.

He was tan, had enough hair for the whole board of

directors and was fit as a cello. Did some jogging in the early morning to get the juices flowing, and after work a couple nights a week worked out those juices on a personal trainer of whom, it was said, he had carnal knowledge.

"Hold the calls, Miss Craig," he said, as the young woman backed out of the room. Do you suppose she sensed my predilection to stare at her sculptured buns? Everything here was a work of art—so much to stare at. The staff, I decided, was selected for their stare appeal, just like Hammurabi's nickels and dimes and Titian's oils.

So you could tell pin-stripe d'Lacy from your run-of-the-mill banker, he wore a gardenia in his jacket buttonhole. I could smell it from where I sat across his Brazilian rosewood desk, which was the genuine article, not the laminate, and was, roughly, the size of Brazil.

I couldn't get over how darn gracious he was. "Are you comfortable in that chair? May I get you something to drink?"

"Thanks, I'm fine."

"Well," he said, taking his measure of me down a nose that could have held its own with the marble statues in the foyer, "Michael Hadaad speaks very highly of you."

I almost fell off my chair. Michael Hadaad? The same guy who tried to clean out my sinuses with a bullet rather than turn over my fee after I had accomplished his goal? He was the last guy in the world I would expect to recommend me.

Michael Hadaad is my pseudonym for this slightly tarnished megabucks who put me through loops on my first case, from which I was grateful to escape with my skin.

d'Lacy seemed amused at my reaction. He was looking at me over the little temple he had made with his manicured fingertips. I could tell he wanted in the worst way to be British. It represented class to him.

"Michael is on our board, you know," he said.

"No, I..."

"Given us a nice piece of change over the years, I daresay."

I nodded. Why else would that creep be on

LAMMA's board of directors?

"Of course, he said you were a rank amateur. 'Childish,' was, I believe, the way he put it. 'A wimp, impossible to reason with'..."

"So why...?"

"Why is obvious, isn't it? You solved his problem. Look here, Yates, I'm a results-oriented guy. I wouldn't have made my museum a world-class institution if I hadn't been. Why, I'd work with a wooden-legged centipede if he brought me the pigeon."

Was there, I wondered, buried in there, flattery?

"He also told me the most remarkable thing about you," he said.

"Oh?"

Franklin d'Lacy nodded. "Said you worked exclusively on a contingency basis." He was especially amused when he said, "Michael quoted you as saying a thousand a day and expenses was tacky."

"Well, perhaps I..."

"That's what interests me," d'Lacy said. "That, and the fact that Michael assures me you are an absolute nut for privacy and secrecy. Discretion, he says, is your byword. No business cards, no office, not even," this he pronounced with relish, "a license."

Was Franklin d'Lacy really winking at me?

"Of course, I understand a contingency fee comes a lot higher than I could buy one of those small-timers, but if you achieve my goal, I will pay you one million dollars."

Also Available from Allen A. Knoll, Publishers
Books for Intelligent People Who Read for Fun

Bluebeard's Last Stand: A Gil Yates Private Investigator Novel
By Alistair Boyle
Mega-priced, contingency private investigator Gil Yates's latest adventure combines a rich widow, a gold-digging boyfriend and a luxury cruise to New Zealand, with all the charm and humor Boyle's fans have come to expect. $20

The Unlucky Seven: A Gil Yates Private Investigator Novel
By Alistair Boyle
Do seven people rule the world? Someone thinks so and is systematically sending bombs to kill each of these seven wealthy and influential men. Three are dead already by the time Yates arrives on the scene. $20

The Con: A Gil Yates Private Investigator Novel
By Alistair Boyle
Gil Yates backs into the high-stakes art forgery world, bringing the danger, romance and humor that Boyle's fans love. $19.95

The Missing Link: A Gil Yates Private Investigator novel
By Alistair Boyle
A desperate and ruthless father demands that Gil bring him his missing daughter. The game quickly turns deadly with each unburied secret, until Gil's own life hangs by a thread. $19.95

The Snatch
By David Champion
Two cops whose methods are polar opposites—in love with the same kidnapped woman—race against time and each other to save her. From Los Angeles' lowlands to its highest mountain, *The Snatch* races at breakneck speed to a crashing climax. $19.95

Phantom Virus: A Bomber Hanson Mystery
By David Champion
Super lawyer Bomber Hanson and his engaging sleuth son take on a dubious doctor. Was young Merilee killed by her prescribed cure? Was it innocent or intentional, or was her diagnosed virus a *Phantom Virus*? $23

Celebrity Trouble: A Bomber Hanson Mystery
By David Champion
Unspeakable accusations of child molestation against mega star Steven Shag prompt him to call Bomber Hanson. Courtroom theatrics abound as the nature of man unfolds in this installment of the acclaimed Bomber Hanson series. $20

The Mountain Massacres: A Bomber Hanson Mystery
By David Champion
In this riveting, edge-of-your-seat suspense drama, world-famous attorney Bomber Hanson and his engaging son Tod explore perplexing and mysterious deaths in a remote mountain community. $14.95

Nobody Roots for Goliath: A Bomber Hanson Mystery
By David Champion
Larger-than-life Attorney Bomber Hanson and his son Tod take on the big guns—the tobacco industry. Is it responsible for killing their client? $22.95

Flip Side: A Novel of Suspense:
By Theodore Roosevelt Gardner II
Can a murder trial really have two such conflicting perspectives? A novel unique in content and format, *Flip Side* gives us two heart stopping versions of the same high-profile multiple-murder case. $22

Order from your bookstore, library, or from Allen A. Knoll, Publishers at (800) 777-7623. Or send a check for the amount of the book, plus $3.00 shipping and handling for the first book, $1.50 for each additional book, (plus 7 ¾% tax for California residents) to:

Allen A. Knoll, Publishers
200 West Victoria Street
Santa Barbara, Ca 93101

Credit cards also accepted.
Please call if you have any questions (800) 777-7623, or if you would like to receive a free Knoll Publishers catalog.